Love Inspired®

A Father's Second Chance

Mindy Obenhaus

Love Inspired®

Uplifting romances of faith, forgiveness and hope.

AVAILABLE THIS MONTH

THE COWBOY'S SURPRISE BABY
Cowboy Country
Deb Kastner

RANCHER DADDY
Family Ties
Lois Richer

FAMILY WANTED
Willow's Haven
Renee Andrews

LOVING THE COUNTRY BOY
Barrett's Mill
Mia Ross

NURSING THE SOLDIER'S HEART
Village of Hope
Merrillee Whren

A FATHER'S SECOND CHANCE
Mindy Obenhaus

ISBN-13: 978-0-373-87978-6

50599

⌂ EAN

LIATMIFC0815

"Your mother told me you were leaving."

As much as she loved her mother, Celeste just might have to wring her neck. "Why would she tell you I'm leaving?"

"Aren't you afraid you'll get bored? Then you'll be stuck in boring little Ouray."

"I happen to love boring little Ouray. *Especially* the boring part."

"Oh, yeah?" He took a step closer, his stubborn stance mirroring her own.

"Yeah." There was barely a hairbreadth between them. He was so close she could smell his soap, feel his breath on her skin.

Her heart raced as his eyes morphed into a deep sapphire and the muscle in his jaw relaxed.

She cleared her throat, dropping her hands to her sides. "Would it…matter if I left?"

His hands dropped, too. "The town would lose their best cook."

"Oh."

"Cassidy and Emma would miss you terribly." His tone was gentle this time.

Caught up in the moment, she threw caution to the wind. She knew she was opening herself for heartbreak but went for it anyway. "And what about you? Would you miss me?"

It took **Mindy Obenhaus** forty years to figure out what she wanted to do when she grew up. But once God called her to write, she never looked back. She's passionate about touching readers with biblical truths in an entertaining, and sometimes adventurous, manner. Mindy lives in Texas with her husband and kids. When she's not writing, she enjoys cooking and spending time with her grandchildren. Find more at mindyobenhaus.com.

Books by Mindy Obenhaus

Love Inspired

The Doctor's Family Reunion
Rescuing the Texan's Heart
A Father's Second Chance

A Father's Second Chance

Mindy Obenhaus

HARLEQUIN® LOVE INSPIRED®

Recycling programs
for this product may
not exist in your area.

LOVE INSPIRED BOOKS

ISBN-13: 978-0-373-87978-6

A Father's Second Chance

Copyright © 2015 by Melinda Obenhaus

www.Harlequin.com

Printed in U.S.A.

Many are the plans in a man's heart,
but it's the Lord's purpose that prevails.
—*Proverbs* 19:21

To the miners of the San Juans,
both past and present.

Acknowledgments

Thank You, Jesus, for using this lowly vessel.

Many thanks to Phil Martinez, longtime miner,
for your willingness to share your knowledge.

To my amazing husband, Richard Obenhaus,
with much appreciation for your love of history.
Only one of the many things I love about you.

Becky Yauger,
I couldn't have done it without you, girl.

Thanks to Ted and Betty Wolfe
and Brandy Ross for all of your help.

Chapter One

Perhaps love wasn't a fairy tale.

Watching the bride and groom share their first dance, Celeste Thompson was taken aback by the longing that filled her heart. She'd never been one to entertain romantic notions. Yet she suddenly found herself wondering what it would be like to be in love. To share your life with someone. To give that person your whole heart.

Celeste froze, the long pearl-handled knife midway through another slice of wedding cake. She could never trust her heart to anyone. She laid the piece of raspberry-filled white cake on a plate. Precisely why she was the caterer, not the bride.

As the romantic ballad came to an end, her eyes again roamed the crowded, dimly lit reception hall in Ouray's Community Center. From all appearances, Cash and Taryn were the epitome of forever and always. Yet how could anyone promise forever? People change. At least that was what her mother said. Countless times. Usually followed by a less-than-flattering remark about Celeste's wayward father.

"Cake, please."

Celeste glanced down to see small fingers gripping

the edge of the lace-covered table. A pair of large sapphire eyes framed by white-blond curls peered up at her.

A smile started in Celeste's heart, spreading to her face. "Well, hello there, sweet girl." The child was adorable, her frilly lavender dress making her look like a princess. "You must be the flower girl."

The little girl nodded, her mischievous grin hinting that she might not be as innocent as she appeared.

"Emma…" A man with dark brown hair and Emma's same blue eyes sauntered toward them. His hands were tucked into the pockets of his tuxedo slacks and his loosened bow tie dangled from beneath the unbuttoned collar of his starched white shirt. Very *GQ*. Tall, dark… Of course, at five foot two, everyone seemed tall to Celeste. One of many reasons high heels were her best friend.

He stopped beside the child. "You've had enough cake, young lady." His baritone voice was firm. Unyielding.

Emma frowned. Her bottom lip pooched out as she crossed her arms over her chest. "Cassidy had two pieces."

"Your sister ate her dinner." The man stared down at her, seemingly unfazed by the pathetic look.

"No fair." The little girl stomped her foot.

He held his hand out to the child. "Let's go see if we can find some more of that brisket. Then we'll discuss cake."

Emma's lip quivered, her eyes welling with tears. Her face reddened and contorted in ways Celeste had never witnessed firsthand. Nonetheless, she recognized the markings of a tantrum. And, from the looks of things, this was setting up to be a good one.

Perhaps she could find a way to change the subject. She opened her mouth, but the man she presumed was Emma's father held up a hand to cut her off.

"I've got this."

Fine by her. After all, Emma was his daughter.

He dropped to one knee. "Emma, please. Not here."

His plea was met with a loud wail.

Celeste bit back a laugh. Seemed the poor man had been through this before.

Pulling his daughter close, he begged her to stop crying. His tuxedo jacket was doing a fair job of muffling Emma's sobs, still…he glanced up at Celeste, defeat and perhaps embarrassment marring his otherwise handsome features.

Surely there was something she could do.

Then again, Emma's father had made it clear he didn't need her help.

The child let out another cry. This time loud enough to be heard over the music.

People started staring.

Celeste couldn't help herself. While she might not be an expert with kids, she'd quelled many an executive tantrum in the boardroom. Perhaps those tactics would come in handy now.

She wiped her hands on a napkin and rounded the table. Knelt beside the pair. "Emma?" She touched the baby-fine curls.

Emma hiccupped then slowly turned her head until her red-rimmed eyes met Celeste's.

"Have you ever had a birthday party?"

The child nodded against her daddy's chest.

"And all your friends and family were there?" She looked at Emma's father, afraid he'd tell her to back off. Instead, he seemed to wait for his daughter's reaction.

Emma nodded again, this time lifting her head.

Celeste continued. "Now, suppose one of your friends got mad and started crying at your party. How would that make you feel?"

The child's eyes darted back and forth across the wooden floor. She wasn't answering, but she wasn't crying anymore, either.

"Would that make you sad?" Celeste offered.

Emma nodded, gnawing on her thumb.

"Well, this is Cash and Taryn's party. You wouldn't want to make them sad, would you?"

Emma shook her head, her eyes growing even bigger. "Tawyn's my aunt."

"I see." She dared a glance at Emma's father. He seemed to have relaxed, though he didn't necessarily look happy. "Well then…" Her gaze shifted back to Emma. "You want to be a big girl for your aunt Taryn, right?"

Emma's smile returned. She nodded once more.

Celeste pushed to her feet.

So did the child's father.

She took hold of Emma's hands and spread her arms wide. "Look at your pretty dress." She let go of one hand and twirled the child with the other. "That's a dancing dress if I ever saw one."

Emma giggled, and Celeste didn't know if she'd ever heard a sweeter sound.

"Now—" stopping, she smiled down at Emma "—do you think you can do what your daddy tells you?"

Emma nodded.

"Good girl. And then, maybe, if it's okay with your mommy and daddy—"

"I don't have a mommy."

Celeste blinked, her cheeks growing warm at the child's candor. "Oh. Well then…" She swallowed, her gaze flitting briefly to Emma's father. "If it's all right with your dad, I can send a piece of cake home with you for later. How does that sound?"

"Yay!" The little girl just about bounced out of her

white patent leather shoes. She tugged her father's hand. "Come on, Daddy. Let's get some more bisket."

"Brisket, sweetheart." As his overzealous daughter pulled him toward the buffet table, he shot Celeste an irritated look. "Thanks for the help. But I can take care of my daughter."

Celeste bristled. She hadn't expected his praise, but she hadn't expected him to be so rude, either. That'll teach her to get involved.

Shrugging off the exchange, she watched the pair walk away. Emma obviously knew she had her father wrapped around her little finger. But did she have any clue how blessed she was to have a father who cared?

I don't have a mommy.

Celeste ached for the child. And wasn't there some mention of a sister?

She shook her head. A single dad with two daughters. No wonder the guy looked defeated. He didn't stand a chance.

"Celeste?"

She turned as Erin, one of her part-time servers, approached.

"We're down to crumbs on the brisket."

"No problem. I've got another tray in the kitchen." Celeste pointed to the cake. "You mind taking over?"

"Not at all." Erin picked up the long knife as Celeste started toward the swinging door. "Sausage is running low, too."

Celeste waved a hand in acknowledgment and continued into the community center's small yet efficient commercial kitchen. The groom's request for Texas barbecue seemed to be a hit with the guests. Good thing Granny had taught her the art of smoked meat. Building the catering side of Granny's Kitchen was important to her bottom line. As were those old hotel rooms over the restaurant.

Donning her oven mitts, Celeste grabbed another foil-covered pan of meat from the oven. The smoky aroma wafted around her as she carried it into the main room. It had taken her all summer to decide how best to address the upstairs units, but she'd finally decided to convert the cluster of six tiny rooms into three large suites. All while remaining true to the building's character and Victorian architecture.

She set the pan into the chafer, thinking of all the beautiful millwork throughout the upstairs space. The wide baseboards and detailed moldings…quality like that was hard to find these days. She could only pray God would lead her to the right contractor. One who didn't cringe when she mentioned the word *salvaging*.

After replenishing the sausage, she topped off the grated cheese and bacon bits at the mashed potato bar, pleased that everything had turned out so well. Word of mouth was a powerful thing, especially in a small town like Ouray.

A popular tune boomed from the DJ's speakers and people flooded the dance floor. Celeste paused to watch. Young and old, everyone appeared to be having fun. Including two little blond-haired girls in lavender dresses. Emma held her daddy's hand, as did the other girl Celeste presumed was her sister.

Although she found Emma's father to be a bit on the arrogant side, the adoring look on his face as he twisted and twirled his two precious daughters around the dance floor melted Celeste's heart. His girls were obviously the center of his universe. And though they were without their mother, Celeste got the feeling that Emma's dad was the kind of guy who would do whatever it took to be both mother and father. He would never desert them, like Celeste's father had.

A sad smile tugged at the corners of her mouth. Those two were lucky girls indeed.

Gage Purcell escorted his daughters, Emma and Cassidy, off the dance floor. In the year and half since his wife, Tracy, had left, Emma's tantrums had grown more and more frequent. Maybe it was a coping mechanism. Maybe she blamed him for her mother's absence. Whatever the case, he needed to find a way to make them stop.

The fact that a total stranger could settle his daughter better than he could had bugged him all night. Not that he wasn't appreciative of the caterer's intervention. The last thing he'd want to do is ruin his sister's special day. Still…

He raked a hand through his hair, eager to call it a night. Dinner and dancing had gone on far longer than he anticipated, though the latter had afforded him some special moments with his daughters. But now that the bride and groom had made their exit…

"Time for us to think about going, too, girls. It's way past my bedtime." Gage wove his daughters between the round cloth-covered tables to retrieve their sweaters.

"But you go to bed after us, Daddy." Seven-year-old Cassidy peered up at him with serious eyes.

"That is true. So it must be way, way, *way* past your bedtimes."

"I'm not—" yawning, Emma leaned against a folding chair "—tired."

He chuckled, knowing his youngest would likely crash before he even put his truck into Drive. Kneeling beside her, he held up her pink sweater. "But your old dad might fall asleep at any—" His eyes closed, he lowered his head and pretended to snore.

Emma giggled. "Wake up." Her tiny hand nudged his shoulder. "Wake *up*!"

"What?" He jerked his head. "I must have dozed off."

Emma shoved her arms into the sleeves of her sweater. "You're silly."

Turning his attention to Cassidy, he held up the purple sweater.

His oldest complied immediately, a dreamy smile lighting her face. "I loved this day."

Standing, he donned his tuxedo jacket and stared down at his two beautiful girls. Their usually straight blond hair had been curled and pulled back on each side and their fingernails were painted the same pale purple as their dresses. "I guess you did. You look like little princesses. And you got to hang with the big girls."

"That was the best part," said Cassidy.

A twinge of guilt prodded Gage. With their mother out of the picture, the girls didn't get to do many girlie things, so he was glad Taryn had included them in all the primping and pageantry that leads up to a wedding.

"Don't forget the cake, Daddy."

He should have known Emma wouldn't forget. He could only hope the caterer didn't.

Taking his daughters by the hand, he started across the hardwood floor.

"Hey there, Gage." His old friend Ted Beatty, a shift supervisor at one of the mines outside town, walked alongside them.

Gage had been trying to get a job with a local mine since moving back to Ouray last year. So far, though, not one nibble.

"Whatcha know, Ted?"

"Not much." He stopped.

So did Gage. He eyed the man who was a little older than his thirty-one years. A deep love of mining and its history had bonded the two from a young age.

"Any hiring going on?"

Ted shook his head, his lips pressed into a thin line. "Don't give up, though, buddy." He gripped Gage's shoulder. "Things could change at any time."

Easy for him to say. Ted had remained in Ouray, getting his foot in the door early when the first gold mine had reopened. Gage, on the other hand, had gone off to Colorado's School of Mines for a degree in mining engineering. If only he'd hung around. Maybe he'd be following his dream instead of biding his time working construction.

"Daddy...what about the cake?" Emma squeezed his hand, bringing a smile to Gage's face.

His girls were the reason he gave up his dream job in Denver and moved back to Ouray. He needed the support of his family. And he'd do it a thousand times over, whatever it took to provide a stable, loving environment for them. He only wished he could say the same for their mother.

He shifted his focus back to his friend. "We're on a mission, but let me know if you hear anything."

"Sure thing, Gage."

Emma skipped alongside him as they continued on to the kitchen. He hoped she wasn't getting a second wind. If that happened, they could be up all night.

He carefully pushed open the swinging door.

"Nana!" Both girls bolted toward a long stainless steel work table as his mother, Bonnie Purcell, stooped to meet them with open arms.

Behind her, the caterer moved aside and busied herself at the sink. But not before her deep brown eyes narrowed on him.

"Oh, my precious girls." Mom embraced her granddaughters. "You were so good today." She released them, smoothing a hand over her shimmering dress as she rose. "Gage, have you met Celeste?" His mother's gaze drifted between him and the caterer, that matchmaking twinkle in her eye.

Man, Taryn hadn't been married but a few hours and his mother had already set her sights on him.

Well, she could try all she wanted, but Gage wasn't going down that road again. He was a failure at marriage and had no intention of setting himself or his daughters up for another heartbreak.

"Not officially." The caterer grabbed a towel from the counter. Chin jutted into the air, she held out a freshly dried hand. "Celeste Thompson. Nice to meet you."

Recalling the irritation that had accompanied his parting words earlier in the evening, he reluctantly accepted the gesture. "Likewise."

Long, slender fingers gripped his with surprising strength.

"Celeste was telling me that she's looking for a contractor to do some renovations in the space above her restaurant." Mom fingered Cassidy's soft curls, her attention returning to the caterer. "Gage has quite an eye for detail."

"Well, it just so happens that I'm a detail kind of girl. I'm *very* particular about how things are done." Her smile teetered between forced and syrupy. "But, if you think you can handle it, you're welcome to come by and look things over."

"Oh, don't be silly." Mom took hold of his daughters' hands. "Gage can handle just about anything." She beamed at Celeste first, then Gage. "Come on, girls. Let's go say good-night to Papa."

The trio stole through the door, leaving him alone with the caterer. Talk about awkward.

She stepped toward the counter and retrieved a disposable container. "Here's the cake I promised Emma. I included enough for you and her sister, too."

He wasn't sure how he felt about that, but accepted the package anyway. "Cassidy."

"I'm sorry?"

"My other daughter is Cassidy. I'm sure she will appreciate the cake every bit as much as Emma and me. Thank you. And…" He forced himself to meet her gaze. "Thank you for helping me out earlier."

"You're welcome." Her golden-blond hair was slicked back into a long ponytail. Save for one wayward strand, which she promptly tucked behind her ear. Her expression softened. "Look, I realize that was kind of an uncomfortable situation with your mother." She peered up at him with eyes the deep, rich color of espresso. "If you'd like to drop by and check out the project, great. However, I understand if you don't have time."

She was actually giving him an out?

He hadn't expected that.

Unfortunately, his finances dictated he not turn down a job. "How about Monday at two?"

Chapter Two

Get in, and get out.

Gage slammed the lid on the aluminum storage box in the bed of his pickup. He really wasn't interested in meeting with Celeste Thompson today. True, his project at the Schmidts' was drawing to a close, and he didn't have anything else on the books, but he was fairly certain that the type of work Celeste wanted was not going to match up with the kind of work he specialized in.

A breeze rustled the golden leaves of an oak in the Schmidts' front yard. Their Queen Anne-style house, with its sprawling porch on the west side, had been one of his favorites long before they hired him to renovate the first-floor bathroom. He loved all the old buildings in Ouray. Appreciated the architecture and intricate details that made them grand. Restoring them was his forte. But he'd encountered one too many city dwellers who didn't see the value in "old stuff." They were only interested in removing the old and making everything modern.

That was like tearing out the heart of a home. Something he could not—would not—do.

He climbed into the cab of his truck, eyeing the burnt-orange landscape that spread up the mountainsides. He supposed it wasn't fair to judge Ms. Thompson based on the actions of others, but she definitely fit the demographic—young urban professionals trading everything for the good life in Ouray, Colorado. What they failed to realize was that while life was indeed good in Ouray, it could also be tough. Many people worked two or three jobs, unless they owned their own business. In that case they had only one job to which they were on call 24/7. Which was why so many people threw in the towel after only one season.

Celeste might be a good cook, but did she have the guts, the tenacity, to embrace Ouray and its oft-difficult way of life? Not to mention its historic architecture.

He fired up the engine and dropped it into gear, deciding he'd find out the latter soon enough.

Heading toward Main Street, he rolled down the windows to take advantage of the mild autumn air. Who knew how many more days they'd have like this? The thirteen- and fourteen-thousand-foot peaks that surrounded the tiny town were already topped with white.

A few blocks down Main, he pulled into a parking spot across from Granny's Kitchen. The place had changed hands several times over the past twenty-some years, but he still remembered it as the Miner's Café. The owner, Mrs. Ward, used to make the best cinnamon rolls he'd ever tasted.

He hopped out of the truck and ambled across the street to the two-story brick and stone Victorian building. Seemed like he'd heard someone mention that Celeste was Mrs. Ward's granddaughter. If that were true, maybe he'd find cinnamon rolls on the menu.

Opening the right half of the wood and glass double door, he was greeted by the most amazing aroma. A colorful dry-erase board to his left boasted tonight's special—

Granny's pot roast with onions, carrots and homemade smashed potatoes.

His mouth watered, the two bologna sandwiches he'd had for lunch a distant memory. He inhaled deeper. Yep, that was pot roast, all right.

Above the menu, a double row of iron hooks lined the wall. Part function, part decor, they were currently home to a well-worn cowboy hat, a fedora that had seen better days and a faded denim jacket.

"Welcome to Granny's Kitchen." Behind the wood-topped counter to his right, Ms. Thompson slid a tray of cookies into a glass case. Her blond hair was again pulled back in a ponytail, her smile easy and relaxed.

"Nice place you have here." He scanned the almost-empty restaurant. Lace curtains covered the lower half of the front windows, adding privacy to the row of wooden booths, while a Texas flag and some old mining pieces adorned the back wall. All in all, the place was warm and homey.

"Thank you." She started to close the case, then paused. "Care for a chocolate chip cookie? They're still warm."

He eyed the treats, his stomach growling. "Sure." He reached for his wallet.

She waved him off, though. "It's on the house." Using a small wax paper sheet, she grabbed a cookie and passed it over the counter.

As promised, it was warm. Not to mention loaded with pecans and some of the biggest chocolate chips he'd ever seen.

He took a bite, savoring the melted chocolate that mingled with a hint of cinnamon. "Delicious." Even better than his mother's. Not that he'd ever admit that to her.

Celeste's smile sparkled in her deep brown eyes. "I do my best to live up to Granny's reputation."

"Hello, Gage."

He turned as the door closed behind Blakely Lockridge, owner of Ouray's finest Jeep tour company, Adventures in Pink. "Hey, Blakely."

His sister's best friend moved toward the counter, a hand resting on her very pregnant belly. "I see Celeste has lured you in with her amazing cookies." She wriggled onto the bar stool beside him, looking like an overinflated party balloon about to pop.

Considering Blakely was down to her last month, her cheerful disposition was a welcome surprise. Tracy, his ex-wife, had been miserable throughout her pregnancies. And never hesitated to let anyone know it.

"You're right on time, Blakely." Celeste pulled another cookie from the case. "They just came out of the oven." She handed it to Blakely. "How are you feeling?"

"Pretty good. The wedding wore me out, but Trent doted on me all day yesterday." She took a bite. "Yum. Did you add more pecans this time?"

"I did." Celeste rested her forearms on the counter.

"This is perfect." Blakely closed her eyes and took another bite. "Just the way I like them."

Gage had to agree. His mother usually left out the nuts, but he preferred them. "Sounds like you're a regular customer."

"Are you kidding?" Blakely smiled up at him. "I've been craving Celeste's cookies and cinnamon rolls for the past three months."

His head jerked toward Celeste. "You make cinnamon rolls?"

"Every morning. Just like Granny did."

"I used to love your grandmother's cinnamon rolls."

"Guess you'll have to stop in and try one then." She regarded Blakely again. "Would you like another?"

Blakely held up a hand. "No, I need to get back to the shop and finish up some stuff before Austin gets out of school." She slid off the stool.

"Speaking of school—" he caught Celeste's attention "—we need to get started."

"Yes." She peered over the stainless steel pass-through into the kitchen. "Karla, I'll be upstairs for a little bit, so keep an eye on things, please."

"What are you guys up to?" Blakely waddled toward the door.

"Gage is here to take a look at the space upstairs." Celeste removed her apron as she rounded the eating counter and dropped it on one of the chairs.

She looked far too dressed up for a diner. He expected casual. But the navy slacks and tailored button-down shirt were more like business casual. He did a double take. Heels? Women didn't wear heels in Ouray.

"Ah, so you finally decided what to do with it?" The two women continued on ahead of him and outside.

"I did. Now I'm eager to get the ball rolling."

Blakely eyed him. "Well, I can tell you that Gage is the best. He did some work on our house and we couldn't be more pleased."

Celeste smiled and nodded. "Guess we'd better have a look then." She turned toward the stairs that flanked the side of the building. "See you tomorrow, Blakely."

He followed Celeste up the old iron staircase. "So is this the only entrance to the space?"

"Yes." She unlocked the door and stepped inside. "I've tried to air it out, but it still has that musty smell."

"Let's hope it's not from water damage." The barely-there foyer was dark and drab, the only light coming from the small window on the door. "Might want to see if we can bring some more natural light in here. Maybe a door with a larger window and some sidelights."

"I was thinking the same thing." Celeste flipped a switch and fluorescent lights hummed down the narrow hallway that spread to the right and left.

He admired the flat-panel wainscoting with bead board insets, certain that beneath the yellowed white paint lay some incredible hardwood. The vintage wallpaper above the wainscoting, though, had definitely seen better days.

"Currently, there are six bedrooms and two baths." She moved down the hallway to the left, opening doors as she went. "My grandparents used it as a bed-and-breakfast."

He peered into the first bedroom, which was big enough only for the full-size bed and small dresser it housed. However, the fluted window trim and rosettes were a welcome sight.

"Here's the first bathroom." She opened a door on the right. "I love the claw-foot tub."

"Do you plan on reusing it?"

"Absolutely." She crossed her arms over her chest. "I want to salvage and reuse whatever possible. So—" her eyebrows lifted in a defiant manner "—if your idea would be to gut the whole place and start fresh, we can call this meeting over."

Call her cynical, but Celeste had no intention of wasting time on another contractor who didn't see eye to eye with her about preserving the character of this space. Ouray's ice festival was only three months away. She'd hoped to have the units ready to lease by then. But by no means was she going to settle for some contractor who didn't give a hoot about the building's history. She knew what she wanted, and she had every intention of getting it.

Gage removed his worn Ouray Mountain Rescue Team

ball cap and scratched his head before tugging the brim back in place. "You do realize this building is over a hundred years old?"

"Part of the appeal."

"That the electrical and plumbing will have to be brought up to code? That can get expensive."

She took a step closer. "I've done my research. However, there are some things I refuse to compromise on." She smoothed a hand over the wide molding around the door. "Like the millwork. Any fixtures that can be reused or repurposed."

"You mean like those?" He pointed to the horrendous fluorescent strips overhead, a smirk firmly in place.

She brushed past him on her way to the door. "If you don't have an appreciation for old buildings and what they have to offer, then I'll find another contractor who does."

"I never said I didn't have an appreciation."

She paused in the foyer and slowly turned to face him. "You didn't have to. Your cavalier attitude said it for you."

Hands resting low on his denim-clad hips, he stared at her with an intensity she hadn't seen before. "Actually, historic buildings are my specialty. I don't believe in wasting, and I'm adamant about remaining true to the architecture."

"You—?"

"Which is why I was quizzing you." He closed the distance between them in only a few steps. "Many people like the idea of a historic building until they find out the cost and time involved. Then they take the easy way out—gut it and start new." He glared at her, his blue eyes darkening to a deep midnight.

Squaring her shoulders, she fixed her gaze on his. "Lucky for you, I'm not one of those people."

"Good. Then it sounds like we're on the same page."

He turned his back to her and wandered down the hall. "If you don't mind, I'll have a look at everything, take some notes and then I need to pick up my daughters."

She followed him. "I believe you're forgetting something."

"What's that?"

"I haven't told you about my vision."

He twisted her way. Quirked a brow. "Your...*vision*?"

"For the new layout. It took me six months to come up with it, but I think it'll work."

"I'll be the judge of that."

Even the most challenging executives hadn't irritated her this much. "Do you plan to fight me every step of the way?"

"No. However, when you're dealing with plumbing and load-bearing walls, you have to be flexible. But, go ahead."

"Thank you. As I was saying..." Over the next fifteen minutes, she did her best to verbalize the image she saw in her mind.

Gage asked questions and voiced concerns. Even made a few suggestions she found difficult to argue with.

"I have a drawing I could give you." She waited by the main door.

"That would be helpful."

She tilted her head to look at him as he rounded the corner. "Just so you'll know, I plan to be heavily involved in this project. I don't want anything to go wrong."

"Neither do I." He looked over his notes. "So if you'll give me your drawing, I will be out of your hair."

She studied him a moment. Despite Gage's appreciation for the architecture, not to mention Blakely's glowing recommendation, Celeste wasn't convinced he was the right contractor for her. How could she work with someone who didn't value her opinion?

Then again, if she wanted these units up and running by January…

"It's in the restaurant." She pushed open the door and stepped onto the small landing. The sun and fresh air were a welcome respite from the stale, musty smell of the long-closed-up space. She continued down the stairs. "When can I expect your quote?"

He followed behind her. "A day or two. Depends how cooperative my girls are."

She could hear the smile in his voice when he mentioned his daughters.

"How old are they?" She faced him as they reached the sidewalk.

"Seven and five."

"Busy ages. I guess they keep you on your toes."

He chuckled, holding the door as she walked inside. "You have no idea."

She retrieved a copy of her drawing from the small office beside the stockroom, remembering the sight of Gage dancing with his daughters. Must be difficult, trying to be both parents *and* run a business. She couldn't begin to imagine. Though she was curious. What would it be like to have a family? Children? Someone who looked up to you and hung on your every word?

We aren't cut out to be mothers, Celeste. She always found it odd when her mother said those words. As though she were apologizing or making excuses. Still, Celeste understood what her mother was saying. Her mother wanted to give her the world. At least the world as Hillary Ward-Thompson saw it.

Shaking off the conflicting thoughts, Celeste returned to the dining room and handed Gage the file folder.

"Would it be all right if I sent cookies for Emma and Cassidy?"

"Oh, man…they'd love that."

She bagged the treats for him.

"What's this?" He pointed to a stack of fliers she had beside the cash register.

"Now that the high season is over and things have slowed down, I thought I'd offer some kids cooking classes."

The look he gave her made her think she'd sprouted horns. "In my experience, kids and cooking don't always go together so well."

Considering Emma's actions the other night, she could understand his skepticism. Though the thought of Emma's mischievous grin made her smile.

"Well, they're not exactly *cooking* classes." She picked up one of the orange fliers and gave it to him, along with the cookies. "Our first one is called Cupcake Mania. We'll provide the cupcakes and icing, and then each child gets to design four custom cupcakes to take home."

"You're talking Emma's language, all right." He studied the paper. "Both girls would be gaga over this."

"Good. I hope you'll consider signing them up, then."

He turned for the door, grabbed hold of the handle. "I'll be in touch."

She watched as he continued past the front windows. How could someone be so infuriating yet so appealing? Gage's disposition left much to be desired. However, the way his face lit up when he talked about his daughters was enough to have women swooning all over Ouray.

Donning her apron, she went to check things in the kitchen. "Are the potatoes on yet?"

"Yes, ma'am." Karla, the closest thing Celeste had to an assistant, looked up from the apples she was peeling for tonight's dessert and pointed to the proofing cabinet along the wall. "And the rolls should be ready to go in the oven any time."

"Perfect." Celeste pushed up her sleeves and headed for the pastry table to roll out the crusts. "Thanks for taking care of that for me, Karla."

"Not a problem."

Celeste's cell vibrated against her hip. She pulled it from her pocket, hating the sense of dread that fell over her when she saw her mother's name on the screen.

"Hi, Mom."

"Celeste, darling. How are you?"

"Wonderful." She sprinkled flour over the table's marble surface.

"You don't sound wonderful. You sound tired." Hillary Ward-Thompson always thought Celeste sounded tired.

"Mom, I'm very well rested." She slept a thousand times better in Ouray than she ever even dreamed of in Fort Worth. "So where are you today?"

"Istanbul."

She balanced the phone between her ear and shoulder. "Hey, if you happen to make it to the Bazaar, pick me up some spices." Of course, her mother rarely did any sightseeing. She was all business, all the time.

"Or you could hop a plane and join me. That way you could pick out your own spices."

Realizing where this conversation was headed, Celeste wiped her hands on a bar towel and wandered into her office. "You know I can't do that, Mom. I have a business to run."

"Celeste, you and I both know a restaurant—especially one in a tiny little place like Ouray—is not where you belong. I didn't bring you up to be slinging hash in some greasy spoon."

She paced beside her desk. Since moving here in April, her conversations with her mother were always the same. Celeste knew beyond a shadow of a doubt that Ouray was part of God's plan for her. Though it definitely was not a part of her mother's plan. "I do not sling hash, nor is Granny's Kitchen a greasy spoon."

"Oh, now you're getting defensive. I'm sorry, darling."

"You're criticizing my livelihood."

"I am not criticizing, Celeste. I'm merely stating facts." *Stay calm. Don't let her get to you.* "You haven't even seen my restaurant."

"Are you forgetting that I grew up in that restaurant? I *know* what it's like." Mom's last sentence held a hint of disdain. She paused for a moment before forging on. "By the way, I ran into Andrew Hemsworth from Golden Triangle Finance the other day. I was telling him all about you and he has a position that would be perfect for you."

"Mom…I'm not interested in any position. I have my own business. I'm happy where I'm at."

"Celeste, you might think you're happy, but you haven't even been through a winter in Ouray."

"No, but I can't wait. I love snow."

"Hmmph."

Celeste took a deep breath and stared at the mountains outside the window. Twin Peaks, was it? She had yet to learn the names of all the summits, but just the sight of them made her frustration wane. "You've got to let this go, Mom. I'm not you. I have to live my own life."

"I know, darling. I just want you to be happy."

Hadn't they just been over this? "I am. Happier than I've been in years."

"If you say so." A moment of silence passed. "Well, I must run. It's late, and I have meetings all day tomorrow."

Celeste knew better than to think her mother was complaining. Mom thrived on those meetings, mostly because she was the one in control. Not to mention good at what she did. Magnet Oil would be lost without her.

"Good night, Mom."

"Good night, darling. Love you." The sound of kisses filtered through the line, just as when she was a little girl.

"I love you, too." Celeste ended the call, her gaze focusing on a worn piece of paper tacked to the bulletin board over her desk.

Follow your dreams. The word *your* was underlined.

After Granny's stroke, she couldn't walk or talk, so when Celeste went to see her, she'd talk enough for the both of them. She'd talk about work and her dislike thereof, the promotion she was up for, but really didn't want. And she'd talk about her dreams. How she longed to escape the big city and find a simpler way of life. A life she could enjoy and call her own.

Apparently Granny's mind had fared better than her body. Because, somehow, she'd managed to scrawl those three words.

Celeste would never forget the look of urgency in her grandmother's eyes when she tucked the note into Celeste's hand. As though it were the most important document in the world.

Perhaps it was.

Since coming to Ouray, the headaches that used to be Celeste's constant companion were history. She looked forward to getting up every morning, no matter how early, because each new day meant she got to do something that she loved.

Yes, Ouray was where she belonged. And she was determined to make this work. Even if she had to work with a cranky Gage Purcell:

Chapter Three

Celeste was getting used to not seeing her condo during daylight hours. Most days she left before the sun came up and returned long after it had gone down. Still, it was home, decorated just the way she liked it. And since it was only two blocks from Granny's Kitchen, her Mustang convertible spent most of the time tucked safely in her garage.

She hugged herself tighter, the gravel road crunching beneath her every step. Tonight seemed particularly chilly. Perhaps it was time to start thinking about wearing something heavier than her jean jacket. Luckily, with the help of Taryn and Cash and their store, All Geared Up, she had a couple of great options hanging in her closet.

By the time her frozen fingers managed to shove the key into the lock of her trilevel condo, Celeste was ready for a hot bath. Her toes were frozen inside her black wedge pumps. Maybe she'd surf the internet tonight for some cute boots. They'd have to be wedges, though. With gravel streets and so many hills, it didn't take her long to figure out that any other type of heel was not practical in Ouray.

She climbed the first set of stairs to the main floor, flipped on the light and tossed her jacket over the arm of the leather love seat before continuing on to the third-floor master bedroom. As water filled the jetted bathtub, she contemplated her meeting with Gage. Attitude aside, the man did seem to know what he was doing. But what if that expertise cost more than she was willing to pay? She'd set a budget. She just hoped it was enough.

I'll be the judge of that. It still irked her, the way he seemed to enjoy challenging her. Then again, she wasn't used to being challenged. She was used to calling the shots. Giving people the information they needed in order to achieve the results she wanted. So if Gage had a problem with that, well…she'd be forced to resort to Granny's method—ply 'em with food. Good food and lots of it.

After a much-needed soak, she padded down to the kitchen in her fuzzy pajamas for a cup of chamomile tea.

"Eww." She set the kettle on the burner, her nose wrinkled. What was that smell? Following the trail of the offending odor, she located its source—the kitchen trash can. Next time she threw away chicken bones, she needed to discard the bag sooner.

She tugged the trash bag out from the wastebasket and cinched it closed as she started down the stairs to the garage. *Note to self—buy an air freshener.*

A sound echoed inside the garage as she opened the door. Like breathing. *Heavy* breathing.

She laughed off the notion, though. This was Ouray, not Fort Worth.

Flipping on the light, she took a step inside and froze. Two weeks' worth of trash was strewn everywhere.

"Oh. My." The breathing hadn't been her imagination.

No doubt smelling the chicken in the bag she carried, the furry black creature turned toward her and snorted.

Panic coursed through her veins. Her hands shook, rustling the bag.

The monster pushed up on its hind legs. Its claws were humongous. Then it roared.

"B-b-bear!" She dropped the bag and rushed back into the house, closing the door behind her. Leaning against it, she could hear the animal on the other side as it ravaged the bag she'd held only a second ago.

What if it got in the house?

She locked the door.

Like that was going to stop him. With those claws, it could probably smash right through the door. She had to get out of here.

Her neighbors. They'd know what to do.

She bolted out the front, across the cold, damp grass, and banged on their door. No answer.

Stepping back, she stared at the darkened house. Only then did she remember the Jacksons were out of town.

She looked around. The house across the street was all lit up. She hadn't met the people before, but this seemed like as good a time as any.

Gravel cut into her bare feet as she crossed the road, but that was nothing compared with what that bear would do if it got ahold of her.

She stumbled up the front steps and knocked on the storm door. Her breaths were coming quick. Too quick. Funny, she'd always been one to remain calm in a crisis. But the sight of those fangs just a few feet from her… White spots darted through her vision.

The door jerked open and Gage Purcell gawked at her as if she was a madwoman.

Then everything went black.

Celeste awakened to find three pairs of blue eyes staring down at her.

She leaped to her feet. Eyes wide, she took in the unfamiliar surroundings—the dollhouse against the wall, the pile of unfolded laundry at one end of the dining table, the two blonde girls watching her every move. "Where am I?"

"In our living room." Gage folded his arms across his chest, his white T-shirt revealing rather large biceps. Couple that with the five-o'clock shadow lining his jaw and he looked like he belonged in a men's cologne ad. "You passed out on our porch."

"I—I did?" She struggled to remember.

"Yes. So I suggest you sit back down. At least until you can get your bearings."

She returned to the tan sofa without argument, her head swimming. "Why was I—?" Then she remembered. "The bear. He—he…how long was I out?"

"A couple minutes." Gage's brow wrinkled as he took a seat in the rocker recliner opposite her. "What bear?"

"In my garage."

"I wanna see the bear." Emma plopped beside Celeste.

Her arm instinctively went around the child's shoulders. "Not this bear, sweetie. He was huge. And his teeth…" She shuddered.

Gage leaned back, crossing one ankle over the other knee. "Ah, it's not uncommon for bears to come wandering into town." His tone was annoyingly nonchalant. "Especially this time of year. Food sources are getting scarce up in the mountains."

She glared at him, her teeth clenched. "It was in my house."

"Perhaps you left your garage door open."

She sent him an incredulous look. "Now, why would I do that? Besides, it hasn't been opened in weeks."

"I meant the back door. As I recall, that whole row of condos—" he pointed in the direction of her house "—has doors on the back of the garage."

"I don't know when I would have opened it. It's been a while since I've even been in there."

"Maybe it wasn't latched properly. The wind probably blew it open."

"That doesn't negate the fact that there's a bear *in my garage*!"

He leaned forward, rested his forearms on his thighs. "Do you have an electric garage door opener?"

"Yes."

"How do you open it?"

"The remote's in my car. There's also a keypad by the garage."

"That's just what I was hoping." He pushed to his feet, wearing a satisfied smile. "All you have to do is open the garage door. The bear will leave, and we can all get a good night's sleep."

She practically had to pick her jaw up off the floor. "What are you? Some kind of nut?"

One dark brow lifted.

"What if the bear comes after me once he leaves the garage?"

"He won't, because you'll be waiting inside the house. Once the bear's gone, you shut everything down."

She rubbed her arms, barely believing what she'd just heard. She couldn't go back over there. Not with that monster on the loose.

Gage raked his fingers through his short hair and let go a sigh. "What's the code?"

"Code?"

"For the keypad."

"You mean you'll—"

"Just as soon as you give me the code."

She chewed her bottom lip. "Um…"

"Great. You don't know it, do you?"

"I do. I just have to remember what it is." She focused on the rustic coffee table littered with cups, papers and crayons.

"Well, if you want that bear out of your house, I suggest you remember."

"I will." She tugged Emma closer, rubbing the soft sleeve of the child's flannel nightgown. "But, in case you haven't noticed, I'm a little freaked out." A feeling she definitely wasn't used to.

He shoved his bare feet into a pair of boots that were next to the door. "By the way, girls, this is Celeste. Celeste, Cassidy—" he motioned to the oldest girl, who sat in the second chair "—and you remember Emma."

The child beside her grinned.

"I like your princess pajamas." Cassidy sent her a shy smile.

Celeste's head dropped in dismay as she surveyed her attire. Being caught in her pajamas was bad enough, but to have Sleeping Beauty, Cinderella and Snow White emblazoned on the front was downright humiliating. Not to mention the pink and blue hearts all over the fleece bottoms.

"5-9-2-7." She jerked her head up.

Gage took a step closer. "Come again?"

She repeated the numbers, slower this time.

"Is your front door open?"

"Yes. But…what if he doesn't leave?"

"He'll leave. I guarantee you startled him every bit as much as he startled you."

"I doubt it," she said under her breath.

He reached for the door. "Girls, you need to get back in bed."

Only then did Celeste realize that her theatrics had probably woken them.

Emma followed him. "But, Daddy, we wanna see the bear."

As much as Celeste wanted to see the bear, too, if only to reassure herself that he was indeed gone, she knew she'd upset their routine. And since tomorrow was a school day...

"Sorry, Emma." Celeste stood. "It's late and you have school in the morning." She laid a hand on the child's shoulder. "You need to do what your Daddy says."

The frowns on their faces nearly ripped her heart out. How did Gage ever discipline them?

"How about I read you a story?"

That seemed to turn their frowns upside down.

"Night, Daddy." Cassidy hugged him first, quickly followed by Emma.

As the two girls started down the hallway off the living room, Gage opened the door.

"I'll try to have them settled before you get back," Celeste said.

He nodded. "Good." Then closed the door behind him.

Gage tromped across the street to the condo he hadn't seen anybody go into or out of in recent months. Ouray was a small town. But what were the odds that Celeste would live right across the street from him?

Roughing a hand over his face, he glimpsed the starry sky. He was never going to get the girls to sleep. They were beyond wired tonight, probably from the cookies Celeste gave them. Which meant he could forget about finishing that quote. Or the laundry. Or anything else, for that matter. And he didn't even want to think about the challenges he'd have waking them up tomorrow morning.

He frowned as he approached the well-maintained condo. If he accepted this project with Celeste, would she bang on his door at all hours of the night, telling him how to do his job?

Surely she wouldn't.

Would she?

Not unless she found another bear in her garage.

He'd never forget the sight of her standing on his front porch, her long blond hair piled precariously on top of her head, eyes big as saucers…right before she passed out.

Not quite the tough facade he'd seen this afternoon. When he carried her inside, she'd looked so…small. Fragile. And smelled of vanilla.

Chucking the annoying thought, he lifted the lid on the remote keypad and punched in the numbers Celeste had given him. He should be at home, making sure Emma and Cassidy were in bed. Not catering to some city girl. He'd done enough of that with Tracy.

Light spilled from the garage as the door began its ascent. Gage stepped inside the front door, only to discover the window was frosted.

He peered down the narrow hall, then up the stairwell. Only one way to get the view he needed.

He climbed the first set of steps and paused at the landing to check the view out of the small rectangular window. Perfect. But what was that loud whistling noise?

With no sign of the bear, he took the second set of stairs two at a time. The beautifully decorated living room stopped him in his tracks, though. Looking at the brown leather furniture with its perfectly placed throw pillows, he felt as though he were invading Celeste's privacy. Like he shouldn't be here.

Probably because he shouldn't. He should be with his daughters. Not leaving them alone with a stranger. And for all practical purposes, Celeste was a stranger. Aside from the fact that she was a good cook, bossy and had an appreciation for historic architecture, what did he really know about her?

Training his ear on that incessant whistling, he whisked past the pristine dining area and rounded into the kitchen. On the stove, steam spewed from the spout of a kettle. He quickly turned it off and moved the kettle to another burner before marching back down to the window without so much as another glance at Celeste's inner sanctum.

He resumed his post just as the bear wandered into the driveway. It was a young one. Not a cub, by any means, but not an adult either. With the whistling silenced, Gage could hear the animal's unhappy grunts, as well as a few of his own.

The bear continued down the street, but Gage watched until it was out of sight before returning to the first level. He hurried past the bathroom and bedroom that were off the foyer then entered the garage via the interior door.

Oh, man. He admired the black ragtop Mustang parked inside. "Talk about a sweet ride." He slowly circled the vehicle, looking for signs of damage. A couple of scratches on the rear bumper but, lucky for Celeste, the canvas was untouched.

Scanning the rest of the single-car space, he shook his head. That bear must have had a good ol' time. And based on what little he saw of Celeste's immaculate house, she was not going to like this. What a mess.

As he suspected, the back door was open. He closed it and twisted the dead bolt, making sure it was secure, then grabbed a lawn and leaf bag from the box on the shelf and started collecting the trash that had been scattered.

Why are you doing this?

He thought about the look on Celeste's face when he explained how to get rid of the bear. Not to mention the way she backed him up when he told the girls to go to bed. Actually, he was kind of surprised she did that. It had been a long time since somebody had his back.

After gathering the trash, he tied the bag and tossed it in the receptacle, making sure to secure the lid. Then he turned out the light and used the keypad to close the garage door before returning to his house.

All was quiet when he stepped inside, so he continued down the hall to check on the girls. Amidst the warm glow of their pink butterfly lamp, he could see that both were asleep. And so was Celeste.

She was leaning against Emma's white headboard, head drooped to one side, with a book in her lap. One hand lay atop Emma's back as the child snuggled beside her.

Something shifted inside him. He longed for his girls to have a mother's nurturing. Someone who did those little things that said, "I love you." Things like reading books, painting their nails and doing their hair. Someone who understood tea parties and Barbie dolls. Someone who was a helpmate to him.

Looking away, he ran a hand through his hair. He wasn't cut out for marriage, though. Even if he was, it certainly wouldn't be with someone like Celeste. She was too much like his ex. Confident, independent, driven... All things that had drawn him to Tracy.

Unfortunately, Tracy had had no interest in motherhood.

Time to get Celeste out of here. He never should have left her with Emma and Cassidy in the first place.

Making his way between the two twin beds, he laid a hand on Celeste's arm.

She didn't move.

He leaned over until his mouth was inches from her ear. "Celeste?" He caught a whiff of vanilla.

A strand of her hair tickled his cheek, causing him to jump.

Celeste did, too. "What are you doing?" Though her words were whispered, they were undeniably sharp.

"Trying to wake you up." He stormed out of the room and busied himself by straightening the living room until Celeste appeared.

"You've got a couple of great kids there." She crossed her arms. "Not one argument. They settled right in and were asleep before I even finished the story."

"I'm glad they didn't give you any trouble." He set the girls' backpacks beside the front door. "You'll be happy to know that your house is bear-free."

"Thank you. You saved my life tonight."

"I doubt that." He darted into the kitchen to dump a handful of string cheese wrappers. "He was just a little guy."

"Little? Not when he was standing on his hind legs, looking me straight in the eye."

He rejoined her. "If he would have been full grown, he'd have been looking down at you." Much like he was right now. When did she get so short?

"I guess I'd better go." She moved to the door. "I really do appreciate you helping me out, though."

He nodded, holding the door open. "Doesn't look like I'll have that quote by tomorrow."

"I understand." She stepped onto the porch and stared across the street. Judging by the way her fingers dug into her arms, she was scared.

He knew he should walk her home. Set her at ease.

But he couldn't. Not while his heart was longing for things that would never be.

He peered up at the darkened sky. "I'll keep watch. Make sure you get home safely."

Her smile lacked its usual confidence. "Okay." She started down the stairs. "Thanks again, Gage. I owe you."

She moved quickly across the street and up her front walk. At the door, she paused and waved before disappearing inside.

He felt like a jerk.

No, he felt like a fool for entertaining such crazy thoughts.

He went back into his house and dropped onto the sofa. He must be tired. But there was no way he'd be able to sleep. He needed to focus on something else.

Standing, he moved to the dining table and opened his laptop. May as well work on a quote. With nothing else in the pipeline, he'd need the work. And, if God didn't want him to have the job, Celeste would turn him down anyway.

But what if He does want you to have this job?

Gage sighed. Then he'd just have to get through it as quickly as possible.

Chapter Four

Gage dropped the girls off at school without a minute to spare. After staying up late to work on Celeste's quote, sleep held him captive with unwanted yet all-too-appealing visions of Celeste with his daughters.

Two cups of coffee and a quick shower later, he was still dragging. He could only hope the breakfast rush went long at Granny's Kitchen. The busier Celeste was, the quicker the process would be. He'd simply drop off the estimate and she could get back to him later. Because after seeing her in his dreams, the last thing he wanted was to spend time in her presence this morning.

A half a dozen cars parked near the corner restaurant encouraged him. He snagged a spot, turned off the ignition and hopped out of his truck.

Despite a clear blue sky overhead, Main Street lay bathed in shadows, waiting for the sun to top the gray, volcanic peaks of the Amphitheater, the curved formation at the town's eastern edge. Frost dappled windshields and rooftops, while the brisk morning air jolted his sleep-deprived senses. A reminder that winter wasn't too far around the corner.

Inside the restaurant, smiling faces and the aromas of

bacon, fresh-brewed coffee and cinnamon transported him to another time. Back when life was simpler and dreams were bigger. When the future was his for the taking. Before reality dealt a heartbreaking blow that would forever change him.

Celeste emerged from the kitchen, carrying three plates. One with eggs, bacon and hash browns, another with what appeared to be breakfast burritos, and the last held a cinnamon roll that looked exactly like the ones her grandmother used to make.

Spotting him, she did a double take. "Be with you in a second."

His insides tensed. While his head told him to drop the file on the counter and run, his stomach begged him to pull up a chair and enjoy a hearty breakfast. Maybe food would help take his mind off last night. If nothing else, it would silence the rumbling in his gut.

He slid onto a bar stool as Celeste moved behind the oak-topped counter.

She paused long enough to grab a coffeepot and a white mug. "You look as though you could use this." She set the cup in front of him and poured.

"That bad, huh?"

She puffed out a gentle laugh. "That bear—or at least thoughts of him—kept me awake half the night, too."

Bear? He palmed the cup, the warmth seeping into his fingers. He should be so lucky.

"Cream or sugar?"

"No, thanks." He took a sip, trying not to make eye contact. Celeste's long blond hair was pulled back yet again, her attire more business than casual, and she'd grown at least two inches since last night.

"Excuse me for a minute." She replaced the coffeepot on the warmer before continuing into the kitchen.

Gage couldn't help wondering what had happened to the overbearing, dictatorial Celeste he met with yesterday afternoon. The one who had been a burr under his saddle. *That* Celeste he could deal with. The sweet, nurturing Celeste who showed up uninvited in his dreams? Not so much.

A few minutes later, she returned, carrying a foil pan encased in a plastic bag. She set it beside him. "My way of saying thank you for your help last night."

The sight of six homemade cinnamon rolls covered in rich, gooey icing wiped every thought from his brain as his stomach broke into a Snoopy dance. "Where's a fork?"

"Not so fast. Those are for later."

"What?"

"Order up."

Celeste reached toward the stainless steel pass-through to the kitchen and retrieved a plate. "This one is for now." Frosting dripped from the steaming, oversize confection she placed in front of him. She handed him a fork and a short stack of napkins. "That is, unless you've already had breakfast."

"I haven't." Filled with more anticipation than a grown man ought to have, he grabbed the fork. "And even if I had…" The warm pastry melted in his mouth while an explosion of cinnamon and creamy sweetness chased his cares away. "This is even better than I remembered."

"I'm glad you approve."

"Oh, I almost forgot." He positioned his fork on the edge of the plate and picked up the file. "I finished your quote."

Her brown eyes went wide. "Are you kidding?" She accepted the folder. "How did you manage that?"

No way was he going to let on how the sight of her

with Cassidy and Emma had affected him. "Guess that bear riled us both."

"Order up."

"Drat!" Celeste tucked the file folder on the opposite work counter, alongside rows of ketchup, mustard and hot sauce bottles. "Duty calls." She retrieved two more plates from the pass-through and was on her way.

Gage savored the first decent cinnamon roll he'd had in twenty years, washing down his last bite with a swig of coffee. Mission accomplished. The quote had been delivered and even though he'd been here longer than planned, the cinnamon roll more than made up for it. Now all he had to do was finish up some last-minute details at the Schmidts' and he'd have the rest of the day to himself.

Standing, he reached for the care package Celeste had given him.

"This is starting to become a habit." Blakely squeezed between him and the next stool, not looking anywhere near as chipper as she'd been yesterday.

He helped her onto the chair. "You feeling okay?"

"Yeah. I just got some disturbing news, that's all." She pointed to the pan of rolls. "Hard to resist, aren't they?"

"Morning, Blakely." Celeste whisked along the other side of the counter.

"Hey there, Gage. Blakely." Kaleb Palmer, Gage's old classmate and the town's most decorated veteran, waited in front of the register.

"I've been hearing some rumors about you, Kaleb." Crossing her arms, Blakely leaned her elbows against the counter and looked past Gage. "And I sure hope they're true."

"Well, that depends." The former soldier who'd lost a leg in Afghanistan grinned and handed Celeste a ten. "What kind of rumors?"

Blakely's brow lifted. "That you're looking to buy Mountain View Tours from Ross Chapman."

Their good-natured friend accepted his change and turned to face them. "Then that would be correct."

"Yes!" Blakely squirmed out of her chair and thrust her arms around Kaleb's waist. "Praise the Lord and hallelujah."

It was no secret that Ross Chapman, Mountain View Tours' current owner, had been a thorn in Blakely's side. Not to mention a poor businessman, nearly running the once well-established business into the ground.

Kaleb squeezed Blakely's shoulder. "I just hope we can be allies instead of competitors."

"Without a doubt. Trent and I will be happy to help you any way we can."

"Good deal." Kaleb started for the door, the hitch of his prosthetic leg virtually unnoticeable. "Now I've just got to get things hashed out with Chapman."

Blakely grimaced. "Don't bring up my name, then. However, I'll definitely be praying for things to work out."

"You can count me in on those prayers," said Celeste.

"Me, too." Gage admired Kaleb's determination and positive outlook. He had every confidence his friend could do wonders for both Mountain View Tours and Ouray's tourism industry.

"'Preciate that, guys." Kaleb waved as he pushed the door open. "Catch ya later."

Celeste grabbed a couple of menus as another couple entered the restaurant. "I'll be right back, y'all."

Gage helped Blakely back into her seat. "That news ought to help shore up whatever was bothering you earlier."

"I wish." She ran her fingers through her strawberry blond hair. "You know the fall festival?"

"Sure. The girls were just talking about it the other day."

"Linda Barrow was supposed to be in charge. I found out this morning that she completely dropped the ball."

He eased back into his own chair, studying Blakely's pinched expression. "What do you mean?"

"You know her mom's been sick."

He nodded.

"Apparently time got away from her. Not one thing has been done for the festival."

"What festival?" Celeste peeled a sheet from her order pad and clipped it to the wheel on the pass-through before giving it a spin.

"The fall festival," said Blakely. "All the churches in town come together to put on a carnival for the kids," Gage explained.

"Sounds like fun."

"It is." Blakely folded her hands atop the counter. "Especially for the kids."

"But it doesn't look like it's going to happen this year." Gage shook his head. "Which is a shame. A lot of kids are going to be disappointed. Mine included."

"No. They're not."

Both Celeste and Gage stared at Blakely.

"Austin has always loved the festival." She absently rubbed her belly, as though considering the child growing inside her, too. "I couldn't bear the thought of losing such a wonderful tradition. So…I said I'd take over."

Gage narrowed his gaze. "At the risk of sounding like Captain Obvious, you do realize you're about to have a baby, don't you?"

Blakely laughed. "Not for another month. The festival will be over long before my due date."

"Still, you can't take this all on by yourself, Blakely. How can I help? Besides sustaining you with cookies and cinnamon rolls."

Their friend grinned. "Well, I wasn't exactly planning on doing the whole thing by myself. Just the organizing. I've got to come up with some people willing to solicit donations of food and prizes, create and set up games, recruit volunteers to work the festival…"

"I can do the recruiting and solicitation." Celeste's expression turned serious.

"You need a bounce house?" Gage downed the rest of his now lukewarm coffee.

"I almost forgot about that. Yes."

"I know a guy in Montrose. I'll give him a call. What else can I do?"

Blakely took a deep breath and smiled, her blue eyes glistening with unshed tears. Probably just hormones, though it still made him uncomfortable. "You guys are amazing. Honestly, I was only coming in here for a cinnamon roll. But you've encouraged me so much." She wiped at a tear. "With the three of us working together, I know we can make this the best fall festival yet."

Together? Gage had no problem with Blakely. But Celeste?

Working on the space above the restaurant, he could do. After all, with Celeste running the restaurant, how involved could she really be in the day-to-day grunt work? But working alongside her on the festival when they butted heads like a couple of bighorn sheep?

What had he gotten himself into?

Gage was the last person Celeste wanted to see this morning. While she was more than grateful for his help last night, she was also embarrassed. What must he think of her, passing out on his porch in her pajamas—princess pajamas, no less—behaving like a crazed drama queen and then falling asleep on his daughter's bed? He probably believed she was downright loony.

And now they'd be working together on a festival? *God, You definitely have a sense of humor.*

"I still have to wrap my brain around all that needs to be done, then I'll lay out a plan of action." Blakely's blue eyes moved from Gage to Celeste. "Think we could meet in a day or two?"

"Should be fine." Gage seemed less than enthused about the prospect.

"Sure." Celeste scanned the restaurant, all too aware that she needed to see to her customers. "Now, about that cinnamon roll?"

"That would make my day, Celeste."

She turned in the order before returning her attention to Gage. "How about you? Another roll? Some protein, maybe? Eggs?"

"No, I'm good. I need to get a move on." He grabbed the pan of rolls and shoved out of his chair. "How much do I owe you?"

"Not a thing. I'm indebted to you for putting up with me last night."

"I guess we're even then." He turned, then stopped. "My contact info is in the file. Just let me know what you decide."

"I will. Thanks again, Gage." Relief washed over her when he walked out the door. If his estimate fit her budget, she was ready to give him the green light and get her "suite" dreams on the path to becoming a reality.

When she looked back at Blakely, her friend was wearing a nice little smirk. "So, just what did Gage have to 'put up with' last night?"

Celeste's cheeks grew warm. "Nothing like you're thinking." She removed Gage's dishes, grabbed a rag from the sink beneath the counter and began wiping.

"Oh?" The arch of Blakely's brow had Celeste blushing all the more. "And what *am* I thinking?"

She halted her cleaning. "Why did nobody tell me that bears roam around town at night?"

Blakely's expression shifted to one of concern. "Why? What happened?"

"I had a close encounter with one in my garage."

"Oh, no. What did you do?"

"I left, of course." She tossed the rag back into the sink and leaned against the counter. "And discovered that Gage lives across the street from me."

Blakely laughed. "What? Did he hear you screaming?"

"I didn't scream."

"Order up."

She grabbed Blakely's order, eyeing the two alongside it. "I banged on his door." Without waiting for a response, she snagged the other orders and was on her way. Not so eager to hear what Blakely had to say next, she refilled coffee cups, delivered tickets and took someone's money at the register while her friend ate.

"I forgot to ask how your meeting went yesterday." Blakely licked a blob of frosting from her fork.

Thank goodness they were off the topic of bears. "Not bad. At least he has an appreciation for historical architecture."

"Do you think you're going to hire him?" There went that grin again.

"Possibly. I can't say for certain until I see his quote." No point in feeding Blakely's sudden impulse to match her up with Gage. Celeste had no interest in being paired with anyone. Least of all, Gage Purcell.

For a Tuesday morning, Granny's Kitchen had enjoyed a steady stream of customers, punctuated by the lunchtime arrival of a busload of senior citizens on a fall foliage tour. Finally, at two fifteen, Celeste had an opportunity to sit down in her office with a chicken salad sandwich and Gage's quote.

Munching on a potato chip, she opened the folder. A detailed spreadsheet showed costs for everything from demolition to labor to materials, as well as estimates for plumbing and electrical. She reviewed the three pages, making note of the lengthy list of variables. Things that could potentially occur that would affect the cost and length of the project.

By the time she got to the end, she feared the project might be out of her reach. So she was pleasantly surprised by Gage's bottom line. Not to mention the estimated completion date—January 1.

Bowing her head, she sent up a brief prayer of thanks. She knew God would send her the right contractor. Now she prayed that God would grant her the grace to overlook Gage's sometimes surly disposition. Especially when it came to her input and expectations.

Finished with her meal, she pulled Gage's business card from the folder. The sooner she gave him the go-ahead, the sooner he could start.

She picked up her cell phone.

"Celeste?" Karla poked her graying head around the corner. "Health inspector's here."

"Now?" She'd been anticipating a visit. And while she had nothing to hide, the timing could have been better.

By the time the inspector—who was very friendly, though a bit chatty—left, Celeste needed to set up for dinner. Thanks to Karla, the Mexican rice was simmering and enchiladas were in the oven, so tonight's special was covered.

Celeste gave the fifty-something woman a hug. "I don't know what I'd do without you, Karla."

"That's quite all right, hon. I didn't do anything you wouldn't do yourself."

Keeping one eye on the restaurant via the pass-through, Celeste grabbed a stack of red plastic baskets and lined each with a wax paper sheet so they'd be ready for tortilla chips later. Granny's Kitchen always had more guests on enchilada night, so she wanted to be prepared. Next, she placed a stack of small bowls beside the baskets. They'd be needed for the salsa she made earlier in the day.

The door swung open then and two little blond-haired girls entered.

Celeste's heart lightened as she rounded into the dining room.

"Celeste!" Cassidy and Emma cheered in unison when they saw her, sending her over the moon with delight.

She gave them each a hug, scanning the area outside for signs of their father.

"We want cupcakes." Emma climbed onto a bar stool.

"No, Emma." Her sister did likewise, though with more finesse. "It's a cupcake class."

"Oh, you mean you want to sign up for Cupcake Mania?" Celeste moved Emma to the center of her seat so she wouldn't fall off.

"Uh-huh." Emma's head bobbed emphatically.

Celeste again watched for Gage. "Where's your father?"

"He's at the hardware store." Cassidy adjusted the plastic headband that held her long hair away from her face. "But he said we could see if you were here."

Something about that statement made her feel warm

and fuzzy. "Well, I'm so glad you did." She contemplated offering them a cookie, but decided against it since it was almost dinnertime.

"It smells good in here." As if to prove her point, Emma took a deep breath through her nose.

"Well, thank you." She patted the child's back. "That's always a good thing in a restaurant."

"Can we eat here?" Emma looked at her, very matter-of-factly.

"I, uh…well…" *Where are you, Gage?* "That would be up to your father. But I'd certainly love to have you." Boy, she needed to stay on her toes around this little one. "So, did your daddy tell you about the cupcake class?"

"No. My friend Bella said she was coming and that I should come, too."

"And me," Emma was quick to inject.

Out of the corner of her eye, Celeste saw Gage walk past the front windows.

He held the door open for Rose Daniels and Florence Griffin. "Ladies."

The two elderly women were always first in on enchilada night. Although Celeste wasn't sure if either one of them actually believed themselves to be elderly. They had more spunk and spirit than people half their age.

"Good evening, ladies." She snagged two menus from beside the cash register.

"You can put those away, Celeste." Rose, Blakely's grandmother and one of Granny's best friends, approached the counter. "Florence and I know exactly what we want."

"Gage, these girls of yours are growing like weeds." Florence fluffed her silvery hair, her hazel eyes bouncing between Cassidy and Emma.

"They sure are." Gage took off his ball cap and ran a hand through his dark hair. "I don't suppose you ladies could give me any pointers on how to prevent that, could you?"

Both women chuckled.

"Just enjoy them while you can," said Florence.

"It was hard to tell you two youngsters from the big girls at Taryn's wedding." Rose's smile reached her warm blue eyes as she regarded the girls. "Did you like getting all dressed up?"

"Yes, ma'am," said Cassidy.

"I likeded the cake best." Leave it to Emma to speak her mind.

Celeste tucked the menus back in their place and followed the women to their usual booth at the center window, so they wouldn't miss anything that might happen outside. "Two enchilada platters then?"

Rose unwrapped the silverware from her napkin, her gaze flitting toward the counter. "Gage always was a handsome one. And there's nothing quite as attractive as a loving father." She looked up at Celeste, the corner of her mouth lifted. "Wouldn't you agree?"

Celeste dared a glance in Gage's direction. "I—I've never really thought about it." Though whenever he was with his daughters or even just talked about them, she saw him in a different light.

Rose studied her for a moment, as though sizing her up. Something Celeste found oddly uncomfortable. "Yes, the enchiladas and an iced tea for me."

She turned to the other woman.

"I'll have tea, too." Florence laid her napkin in her lap.

"All right, then. I'll be back in a sec." Celeste dropped off their order, added chips to a basket and salsa to a bowl, then filled two clear plastic cups with fresh-brewed iced tea and topped them with a lemon wedge. After delivering them to Rose and Florence, she made her way back to Gage and the girls.

"Daddy, Celeste said she'd *love* it if we'd eat here. So can we? Please...?"

Heat crept up Celeste's neck. She was tempted to clarify Emma's statement, but refrained.

"Well, given the fact that I haven't even thought about dinner and enchiladas sound *really* good, I suppose we could stay."

Cassidy sent her father a look that was far too serious for a seven-year-old. "Don't forget about the cupcake class."

"Oh, yeah." He looked at Celeste. "I need to sign these two munchkins up for Cupcake Mania."

"Great." She reached behind her for the notepad she used for registration. "We are going to have so much fun." She wrote down their names, eyeing Emma and Cassidy. "So what's your favorite cake flavor?"

"Chocolate!"

"Strawberry." Though her blue eyes were wide with excitement, Cassidy's response was much more subdued than her sister's. She was definitely the more insightful of the two. Not quick to act. She pondered things.

"In that case, there should be something for both of you." She rang up the registrations. "I'm glad they're coming."

Gage pulled out his wallet and handed her the payment. "Once Cassidy got wind of it from her friend at school, there was no other option."

She peered up at him. "I looked over your estimate."

His sapphire eyes seemed to smile with anticipation, unleashing an odd sensation inside her. Perhaps it was Rose's words that had her off-kilter, but she suddenly found herself second-guessing her decision to hire him.

Not only did he challenge her plans and opinions, she had the strangest feeling he posed a threat to her heart.

Yet before she could think better of it, the words tumbled out of her mouth.

"How soon can you start?"

Chapter Five

Gage scanned the dark, narrow space above Granny's Kitchen, the thrill of another transformation pumping through his veins. He loved every new job and the prospect of what lay ahead. Repurposing old buildings was a lot like mining. You never knew what might be hiding just beneath the surface. Buried treasure? Or something that should have remained hidden?

After getting the go-ahead from Celeste Tuesday evening, he and Logan Hancock, his hired helper, came in Wednesday to take out all of the furniture, the bathroom sinks, toilets and bathtubs. Today the real work began.

Since they were going to reuse the original trim, they had to remove all of the old millwork before they could take down any walls. That took time, carefully unseating each piece from its century-old resting place, then sorting, labeling and stacking it to be used later. If they didn't do things right, they'd be left with a lot of heartbreak, splintered wood and a large bill at the lumberyard.

Fortunately, he'd done enough renovations to master what was once a daunting task. And Logan was getting there. Armed with pry bars and hammers, Logan tackled one of the guest rooms while Gage completed the foyer and hallway. He was starting on another of the guest rooms when he heard Celeste call his name.

"In here."

Decked out in her high heels and a pair of dressy gray slacks, Celeste tiptoed through the dust and debris. He relished the sight, storing it in his mind's eye, ready to pull out whenever the all-too-perfect image of a sleeping, nurturing Celeste decided to taunt him.

Appearing a bit confused, she looked at him. "There are still walls."

Though a statement, he didn't miss the underlying question.

"Yes." He glanced at the obvious. "Yes, there are."

"But I thought you were going to remove them."

"Eventually. If we do that first, though, we risk damaging the millwork."

Her mouth formed an O as realization dawned.

He picked up a baseboard, turning it over to the unfinished side. "Look at this hundred-year-old hardwood." Stepping closer, he smoothed a calloused hand over the surface. "You won't find wood of this quality these days."

"Why not?" Her espresso eyes were filled with wonder.

"The trees they used for timber were a lot older back then." He pointed to the dense grain. "See how tight these rings are?" He knocked it with his knuckles. "This is some hard wood."

A smile played at the corners of her mouth. "That's good, right?"

"Very good."

She stepped back. "Say, uh, on your quote, you had an estimated completion date of January 1. Do you still stand by that?"

Sooner, if he had his way. "Barring anything unforeseen."

Her smile grew bigger. "Good." She scanned the tiny room with its worn-out emerald green carpet and he wondered if it was simply a parting glance or if she planned to change something. "I guess I'll let you get back to work then." Turning, she disappeared into the hall.

That was easy. He shoved the pry bar behind another molding. He halfway expected her to tell him how to do his job or want to help. Maybe it was a good thing she dressed the way she did.

He'd barely pried the wood loose when Celeste appeared again.

"Are you keeping track of which trim goes where?"

He should have known better than to think he'd get off without some questions. "We label every piece."

"And your helper is doing the same thing?"

Letting go of the pry bar, he stood. "Logan knows what he's doing. I wouldn't keep him around if he didn't."

"Good. Good." Her gaze traveled down the hall. "Where are you putting the wood?

He pinched the bridge of his nose. *Help me, Lord.* "For now, we're stacking it in one of the other rooms. I don't want to put it outside and risk getting it wet."

Her brow furrowed. "No, I suppose not." She remained silent and he feared what might be going on in that pretty head of hers.

"Anything else?" He knelt again, his hammer at the ready.

Her lips pursed as she shook her head. "Not that I can think of." She shrugged. "Carry on." With that she was gone. Though this time he waited until he heard the door close to resume working.

Energized by a healthy dose of country music, he completed two more guest rooms before Celeste interrupted him again, shortly before lunch. She coughed as she approached, waving a hand in front of her face.

He finished marking the door trim that was in his hand. "This is nothing. The dust will really be flying once we start knocking down walls."

She stood in the threshold of the tiny guest room that faced Main Street. The late morning sun filtered through the windows, highlighting a million tiny particles hovering in the room. "And when might that be happening?"

"Later this afternoon. Maybe." Using the sleeve of his denim work shirt, he wiped the sweat from his brow. "We're about done with the trim. Then we'll need to pull out the carpet."

"Good. I know you have an order in which you need to do things, but I can't *wait* to get a feel for how things are going to look."

"I understand." He'd be the same way. He eyed the two interior walls. Just getting rid of one would open things up. Perhaps he'd consider throwing her a bone.

"I made a quick run to the hardware store." In her hand, she fanned out several paint chips. "What do you think? Should I go with a gray-toned neutral or stick with your basic off-white?"

Women. Only a few hours into the job and she was ready to decorate. "It's a little early to be thinking about paint."

"I know, but I'm getting restless. It's part of the big picture, you know?"

"Oh, I get it. Still, there are some things you're going to want to consider." He pointed to the south wall with its drooping wallpaper. "This building is made of stone, so you might want to think about keeping some of the exterior walls exposed."

"Ooh, great idea." Her face lit with excitement. "The stone will add some rustic charm."

"Yep. And you wanted to remain true to the character of the building."

She slid the paint colors back into one neat stack. "I guess I'll just have to wait, then." She peered up at him through those long lashes. "Not that it'll be easy."

"Anything worth waiting for never is."

Her cell phone rang and she pulled it from her pocket. "Hey, Karla." She paused. "Okay, I'm on my way down." Tucking her phone away, she looked at him. "Lunch crowd is starting to arrive."

"That late already?" He eyed his watch. Eleven forty. "Guess I'd better get a move on. I've got plenty to keep me busy." He headed into the hallway, hoping she'd take a hint. The more times he had to stop and cater to her, the longer this project was going to take.

She smiled and headed for the main door. "I know you do." She shoved it open. "I'll check in with you later."

He could hardly wait.

Lucky for him, lunchtime in the restaurant must have been busy. Now, as Logan carried rolls of worn-out, nasty carpeting to the Dumpster outside, Gage set his sights on a wall between one of the bathrooms and a guest room. Given the musty smell that permeated the entire space, he suspected water damage.

After donning a dust mask, he butted the wall with a sledgehammer, crumbling the plaster. A few more blows and he was able to get at the thin, narrow strips of wood behind it with a pry bar.

"Dude, you started without me."

Gage eyed his helper. "Grab a mask."

Logan complied, then picked up the discarded sledgehammer and continued to send dust flying while Gage pulled off the laths between the studs.

When they exposed the plumbing, he motioned for Logan to back off. "I was afraid of that."

He snagged the flashlight from his back pocket and moved in for a closer look. Plaster dust swirled around him, coating his safety glasses. He wiped it away.

"Gage?" Celeste's voice trailed down the hall. The woman had terrible timing.

Lowering the light, he met her at the door.

"There you—" Her smile evaporated, her gaze narrowing. "What's wrong?"

Moving past her, he grabbed another mask from the box and handed it to her. "Put this on."

"Why?"

"Just do as I say." The words came out harsher than he'd intended.

Celeste scowled, but obeyed, staying with him as he reentered the guest room.

Her smile returned when she saw the partially demolished wall. "I thought things had gotten noisier up here." She visually traced the opening. "It feels bigger already."

"Did you happen to look over that list of variables I included in my quote?"

"Yes." She shifted from one foot to the other. Crossed her arms over her chest. "Why? What's the problem?"

"Asbestos."

A flood of emotions played across her face as she processed the word. Disbelief, fear and, finally, resignation.

"We can't do anything else until we get a removal team in here." He didn't like saying it, but it had to be said. "And it won't be cheap."

Contemplative, she nodded, chewing her bottom lip.

"Are there people in the area who can do this sort of thing?"

"There's an outfit in Montrose I've used before."

"How long will the removal take?"

"A couple days to a week. Just depends how much there is."

"And you can't do *any* work until they're done?"

He shook his head, surprised at how well she was taking things. "Not until they've tested the air to make sure we're clear."

"How soon do you think they can get out here?"

"Won't know until I call them."

"Then let's go ahead and do that."

"I'll get right on it." Of course, it was already Thursday, so he doubted they'd be able to get anyone out before Monday.

Holding a hand over her mask, Celeste moved in for a closer look.

He pointed to the wrapped pipes. "This is the problem area."

"What about the restaurant? Will it be affected?"

He had a feeling her calm demeanor was about to change. "That'll be up to the inspector." His gaze met hers. "But you might have to close for a while."

Celeste dunked the bag of herbal tea into the cup of hot water, feeling as though she was in a daze. News that she might have to close the restaurant, even for a short time, had kept her awake much of the night.

Her gaze traveled over the cozy dining room. Until six months ago, she hadn't laid eyes on it in over twenty years. But the moment she did, something sparked to life inside her. A feeling she'd never experienced before. As if she was home.

Since then, Granny's Kitchen had consumed her every thought, and nearly every waking moment had been spent here. What would she do if they forced her to close her doors?

At least the inspector wasn't due until Monday, which meant Cupcake Mania was safe. Good thing, too. What she'd originally conceived as a small class for kids had turned into a full-blown event. Since they were making the cupcakes, filling and frostings anyway, Karla suggested they make extras to sell. After all, cupcakes were all the rage, yet no one in Ouray sold them. If she had to cancel…

Cease striving, and know that I am God.

The verse from Psalms played across her heart, imparting peace into her spirit. She'd trusted God when He'd nudged her to take ownership of Granny's Kitchen. And she would trust Him now.

She scooped the cup and saucer in one hand then grabbed a platter of glazed vanilla scones, miniature cinnamon rolls and some sliced fruit with the other and made her way to the booth where Gage and Blakely were already engaged in conversation. Hopefully the lull between breakfast and lunch would last long enough for the three of them to make some much-needed progress on the fall festival.

"Here you go." She set the tea in front of her friend, eyeing Gage's half-empty coffee cup. "Care for a refill?"

He held up his hand. "No, I'm good."

"These look delicious." Blakely selected a petite scone and set it on one of the three small white plates Celeste put out earlier.

"I know what I'm going for." Gage snagged a roll.

Celeste scooted in beside Blakely and picked up her plate. "Since I haven't had any breakfast, I'll take one of everything." She'd been too wound up to eat earlier. But now that God had reminded her Who was in charge, her appetite returned with a vengeance.

They ate in silence for a moment. Finally, Blakely wiped her hands on a napkin and opened up the spiral notebook she'd brought with her.

"I came up with a list of games." She laid the notebook in the middle of the table. "You guys are welcome to add or delete whatever you like." Using her pen as a pointer… "The cake walk is always popular." She glanced between Celeste and Gage. "But we'll need people to donate baked goods."

Celeste gestured to the platter between them. "You know you can count on me."

"My mom's always happy to donate."

Blakely grinned. "And with her new kitchen, I'm sure Taryn will welcome any excuse to bake."

"Add in all the ladies from the churches and I think we're covered." Celeste popped a strawberry in her mouth.

"Good point." Blakely continued down the list. "The little ones like the lollipop tree. They haven't had it in a few years, though. Apparently the tree got lost somewhere along the line."

"I can make a new one." Gage reached for a second roll.

Blakely eyed him. "Could I talk you into making a backdrop for the beanbag toss, too?"

"Sure. While I'm at it, may as well make one for the football toss. That tends to draw the older kids." He grinned. "Especially the boys trying to show off for the girls."

"Or vice versa," said Celeste.

The playful look Gage sent her made her squirm. As

though he'd just uncovered some deep, dark secret she'd been withholding.

"That explains a lot." Eyeing her over the rim of his mug, he took a swig of coffee.

Clearing her throat, she returned her attention to an amused Blakely. "What other games did you have in mind?" She focused on the list. "A tug-of-war?"

"Yes. Boys against girls, policemen against firemen." Blakely reached for a melon slice. "But the competition between moms and dads is always the high point of the day."

"Sounds like fun." Excitement bubbled inside Celeste. Growing up in a large suburb outside Fort Worth, she missed out on the sense of community that came from living in a small town. True, there were smaller communities within the large, like churches and schools, but the idea of an entire town banding together for a single event was something she'd never been a part of—until she came to Ouray.

"Gage—" Blakely shifted her attention "—did you talk with your friend about the inflatables?"

"Not yet." He pulled his cell from the breast pocket of his T-shirt and began to type. "But I'm making a note to do it this afternoon."

"Great."

Before he could finish, his cell phone rang. Confusion seemed to knit his brow as he looked at the number. "Excuse me, ladies." He pushed out of the booth. "Hello?"

"I'll make some calls next week, see if I can't drum up volunteers and donations." At least it would keep her busy while the restaurant was closed. Give her a sense of purpose instead of hanging around her condo in her pajamas.

"Excellent. Tell the volunteers we'll plan a workday for next weekend." Blakely pulled some folded papers from the front of her notebook and handed them to Celeste. "Here's a list of businesses that have made donations in the past. Things like candy and small trinkets for prizes, food and drinks for concessions—"

"What kind of food do y'all usually have?"

"The typical fair-type stuff. Burgers, hot dogs, nachos—"

"Celeste?"

She looked up as Gage slid in across from them again.

"That was the inspector. He's had a cancellation, so he'll be here at one o'clock."

"Inspector? For what?" Blakely's gaze darted between them.

"Asbestos," Gage offered before she could respond, which was probably good since she was still reeling from his announcement. What if they shut her down today? Cupcake Mania had a full slate of attendees. It would break her heart to cancel.

"Oh." Blakely nodded. "Well, it's not like you're the first one to deal with it. With all of our historic buildings, it's kind of commonplace."

Celeste folded her hands atop the table. "I suppose. But dealing with it sure is going to be a pain. According to Gage—" she nodded in his direction "—I might even have to close the restaurant."

"What? They can't do that. Where else will I get my cinnamon roll and cookie fixes?" A smile broke through Blakely's serious expression. "I'm only half kidding, you know."

Celeste patted her hand. "Don't worry. I'm sure I can keep you covered."

Blakely grimaced then, reaching a hand around to her back.

"You okay?"

"Yeah. Trent says it's Braxton Hicks contractions."

"Ah, yes. False labor. I remember it well."

Both Celeste and Blakely sent Gage a curious look.

"Not from personal experience. Tracy had them with Emma."

Celeste knew nothing about pregnancy and the kinds of things a woman went through. Yet, despite her mother's insistence otherwise, it was something she one day hoped to experience. Of course, to do that she'd need a husband. Someone she loved and trusted with her whole heart.

Just thinking about it made her palms grow sweaty.

Perhaps her mother was right.

Celeste was better off alone.

Chapter Six

The cold, rainy weather outside Saturday did little to dampen Celeste's spirits. The inspector had confirmed that she would have to close during the asbestos removal—not to mention remove everything from the restaurant. However, the process wouldn't start until Monday. So not only was Cupcake Mania a go, it was on its way to being a huge success.

"This was a wonderful idea, Celeste." Gage's mother, Bonnie, took the linen napkin from her lap and laid it on the table. She'd brought the girls for the class, but decided to stay. "Not just for the kids, but to have an afternoon tea on a day like today…" Laying a hand to her chest, she let go a satisfied sigh. "Such a treat. And that double dark chocolate cupcake was to die for."

Comments like that always made Celeste smile. "I'm glad you enjoyed it." She glanced around the dining room. She'd never seen the place so crowded at three in the afternoon. Thank goodness she'd had the foresight to bring in extra waitstaff. "It has been fun."

"Fun? This is downright delightful. Talk about a nice change of pace." Bonnie brushed her dark brown bangs to one side. "You should consider doing this more often."

Given the overwhelming response, she'd been contemplating the same thing.

Turning in her seat, Bonnie watched the ten children huddled around the long plastic-covered table in the center of the dining room.

Heather, Karla's daughter, helped Emma swirl the buttercream frosting atop her latest masterpiece. Celeste had hired the teenager to assist with the kids. After all, with decorator bags full of frostings and fillings, they were only one squirt away from disaster.

"Just look at how focused they all are." Bonnie draped an arm over the back of her chair. "I was afraid it might be chaos in here, but they've been so well behaved."

"Honestly, I'm a little surprised myself. I mean, there's been just as much frosting going into their mouths as there has on the cupcakes."

They shared a laugh.

"Would you like me to take this stuff out of your way?" Celeste gestured to the tea service on the table.

"Yes, please." Bonnie stood. "I need to visit the little girl's room anyway."

After clearing the table, Celeste went to check on her budding pastry chefs. She couldn't have asked for a better group of kids. Even the two reluctant boys whose mother practically dragged them in seemed to be enjoying themselves. The younger of the two had chocolate frosting smeared across his left cheek and his tongue peeked out the corner of his mouth as he added an abundance of colorful sprinkles to his chocolate creation.

On the other side of the table, Cassidy applied pink sugar pearls one by one to a strawberry cupcake topped with white buttercream frosting.

Beside Cassidy, her friend Bella squeezed violet-tinted buttercream onto a third chocolate cupcake. Obviously

Bella was a girl who knew what she liked and would not be swayed otherwise.

Shifting her attention to Emma, Celeste noted that the child had grown uncharacteristically quiet. Her face was a little flushed, too.

She rounded the table to check on Gage's youngest, but Bonnie cut her off.

"Celeste, we have a *little* problem." She pulled Celeste aside and leaned closer. "One of the toilets is overflowing in the ladies' room," she whispered.

"What?" Celeste jerked her head in the direction of the bathroom.

"I tried to turn off the water but the valve wouldn't budge."

Pushing up the sleeves of her sweater, Celeste strode toward the restroom with Bonnie close on her heels. Inside, water poured from the handicapped stall, covering the hexagonal floor tiles and drawing closer and closer to the door. She tiptoed as quick as she could through the water and into the stall. Reaching behind the commode, she gripped the oblong-shaped handle.

Righty tighty, lefty loosey.

She turned the handle clockwise. Or attempted to, anyway. "I can't get it either." Maybe the old adage didn't apply to toilets. Just to be sure, she tried counterclockwise. Nothing.

Tiptoeing back out, she looked at Bonnie. "I'm going to need a plumber."

"Nonsense." Bonnie placed an arm around Celeste's shoulder and escorted her in the direction of the door. "I've already called Gage. He'll be here in just a minute."

Celeste pulled free, turning back into the flooding bathroom. "I don't have a minute." By then the water would be drenching the carpet in the dining room. Carpet that was only six months old.

"Honey, a plumber couldn't get here any quicker."

Pliers. She needed pliers.

She swept through the dining room, kitchen and into her office. She knew this tool kit would come in handy someday. Picking up the prepackaged case, she thumbed the latches open and lifted the lid.

"Aha!" Pliers in hand, she marched back to the bathroom. She could do this. She *had* to do this.

As she crouched between the toilet and the wall, water splashed onto her arm. She shuddered. Thank goodness it was coming from the tank and not the bowl. Still, the wetter her toes became, the more grateful she was for her sparkling clean bathrooms.

She fumbled with the pliers before getting a decent grip on the metal valve. Using both hands, she twisted.

"Any luck?" Bonnie's voice came from the bathroom door.

Celeste grunted. "Not yet."

"Oh, hallelujah."

"What?"

"Gage just pulled up."

Hearing the door swing shut, Celeste gripped and twisted one more time. The thought of Gage coming to her rescue once again held about as much appeal as the toilet water that continued to soak her sleeve.

"Whoa…looks like I should've brought a paddle." Gage sloshed in behind her and held out a hand.

Reluctantly, she took hold, trying not to notice the way his muscles strained the fabric of his flannel shirt as he lifted her to her soggy feet.

Ignoring the sudden pounding of her heart, she glanced

toward the door to see where the water was now. "The valve must be rusted open." Right at the threshold.

He moved into the stall and bent to try the valve. "Yep, it's definitely rusted." Straightening, he faced her again. "I'll have to cut off the water at the main valve." He started into the dining room. "Better let the kitchen help know."

"Of course." She followed him, pausing at the counter. "How long will the water be off?"

"No more than an hour, if that. It's an easy fix."

She lowered her gaze. After all the bad news she'd had lately, she liked the sound of that.

"Hey." He locked a finger under her chin and coaxed her to look at him. "Everything will be just fine. I'll take care of the plumbing. You take care of Cupcake Mania."

The unexpected, almost intimate gesture sent a wave of awareness racing through her. His smile was as comforting as Granny's old quilt. His midnight eyes invited her to trust him.

He lowered his hand and she found herself missing his touch. "Looks like you've got quite a crowd."

She tried to speak, but her mouth had gone drier than the Sahara.

Snap out of it, Celeste. He's just giving you some friendly encouragement. Don't read things into it that aren't there.

She pried her tongue from the roof of her mouth. "Yes. The response has exceeded my expectations." She watched another trio of ladies enter. "So, about that water…"

"I'm on it." With that, he was out the door.

Eyeing the stack of bar towels beneath the counter, she grabbed one, toweled off her sweater and washed her hands. Then she grabbed three menus, including printouts of the special Cupcake Mania menu, which included afternoon tea, and went to greet her new arrivals.

On her way back to the kitchen, she spotted Bonnie near the front door.

Gage's mother waved. "Thank you for a delightful afternoon, Celeste."

"See you soon, Bonnie." Between customers and kids, Celeste managed to stay busy, keeping her mind off Gage and the faulty toilet. That is, until she saw him carrying an industrial-sized vacuum through the dining room.

"Water's back on," he said as he passed the kids table. "Soon as I get the water out of there, the ladies' room will be back in business."

"Where's my daddy going?" Emma leaned against Celeste's hip, her voice sounding as if she might cry.

"He's just fixing something for me, sweetie." Heat penetrated Celeste's skin as she tugged the child closer. "Baby, are you okay?" Dropping onto one knee, she laid the back of her hand against Emma's pink cheeks.

"I don't feel good."

"Oh, sweetie, I'm sorry." Celeste laid the child's head against her clean shoulder, longing to pull her into her lap. "Why don't I get you a cool rag?"

"I want my daddy."

Celeste's grip instinctively tightened as memories drifted to the forefront of her mind. Since her mother was always traveling, her father had been the one to take care of Celeste when she got sick. She could still remember the gentleness of his strong hands as he stroked her back.

The first time she took ill after her parents' split, Granny was the only one there. And while Celeste loved her grandmother and knew Granny had her best interests at heart, it wasn't the same. She wanted her daddy. But he either couldn't or wouldn't come.

"Okay, baby." She settled the child back into her chair. "I'll be right back."

She marched across the dining room and pushed open the bathroom door. The loud whir of the shop vac filled the air. "Gage?"

His back to her, he was oblivious.

She'd need a megaphone to be heard over this racket. In the meantime, his daughter was feeling worse by the minute.

Locating the switch on the canister, she turned the power off.

He whirled around and spotted her. "Oh, hey. Didn't see you there."

"Emma needs you."

"Okay. Tell her I'll be right—"

"No, Gage. Your daughter needs you. *Now.*"

No man should have to endure this many episodes of *My Little Pony*. But, at this point, Gage would do just about anything to make his baby girl feel better.

Trying to ignore the mindless chatter coming from the television, he perched on the edge of the sofa, beside Emma. Her long blond hair spread over the pink pillow he'd brought from her bed.

"How about some chicken noodle soup?"

She pulled her favorite unicorn blanket, the one she'd had since she was a baby, up to her chin, frowned and shook her head.

"You need to eat something, sweetheart." He stroked her arm.

She started to shake her head, then grinned instead. "Cupcake?"

So the Tylenol *had* taken effect. Yet for as much as he wanted to give in... "Emma, your body needs good stuff to make you feel better."

"Cupcakes are good."

"They taste good, yes, but they don't have the vitamins and minerals to help your body heal." He supposed canned soup didn't offer a whole lot more, though he wasn't going to let her know that.

"I don't want anything to eat." The words were almost a sigh. She slung an arm over her head and focused on her show again.

He'd have to try again in a little while.

Standing, he retreated to the kitchen, glancing at the large round wall clock as he went. Six thirty. No wonder his stomach was complaining. After an early lunch, he hadn't even had time to snag a cupcake at the restaurant.

He opened the refrigerator, then the freezer. He should have made a grocery run to Montrose today instead of putting it off until tomorrow. Of course, he'd also contemplated eating dinner at Granny's Kitchen, but with Emma sick, that wasn't happening. Too bad Celeste didn't deliver.

Thoughts of Celeste gave him pause. After his mother called, he'd grumbled all the way to the restaurant. Playing hero to Celeste once this week was enough for him. But when he entered that bathroom and discovered her crouched beside the toilet, water dripping on what looked to be a very pricey sweater as she tried to turn that valve, a strange tightness wrapped around his heart. In some odd way, he found the sight almost endearing. The fact that she was willing to roll up her fancy sleeves and do what needed to be done scored points in his book.

But why was she so adamant, almost rude, when she realized Emma was sick? She wouldn't even let him finish vacuuming the water from the bathroom. Did she think he'd expect her to take care of his daughter or that he wasn't capable? Maybe she couldn't tolerate kids. Though, from what little interaction he'd witnessed between Celeste and his daughters, he knew that wasn't the case.

Still, the urgency, almost panic, was something he wouldn't have expected from her.

A knock sounded at the front door.

"Daddy..."

"I heard it, sweetheart." He crossed in front of the TV. Poor kid. Any other time she would have bounded off the couch and beat him to the door.

Outside the window, the glow of a floodlight revealed that the heavy rains of this afternoon had morphed into a steady drizzle. He reached for the knob and pulled the door open.

His heart skidded to a stop when he saw Celeste standing on the front porch.

Wearing an uncertain smile, she lifted a hand to slide the hood of her raincoat back, allowing her long golden ponytail to tumble over her shoulder. In her other hand, she carried what looked like a picnic basket.

He pushed open the storm door.

"How's Emma?"

"Thanks to Tylenol, her fever is on its way down. At least for the moment." He made a quick glance over his shoulder. "And *My Little Pony* seems to be helping, too."

That earned him a real smile. "Always worked for me." She gestured at the basket. "I brought her some of Granny's chicken soup. Guaranteed to cure almost anything."

He hoped Celeste's offer would elicit a more favorable response than his. "Come on in." Moving aside, he held the door as she passed.

Emma's eyes widened. "Celeste!" She started to hop up, but Celeste intercepted her, gave her a quick hug and encouraged her to lie back down.

While his daughter's reaction didn't surprise him, it

did worry him. He didn't want either of the girls forming any kind of attachment to Celeste. After all, he had no intention of getting married again, to Celeste or anyone else.

Celeste glanced around the room. "Where's Cassidy?"

"Spending the night with my folks."

"That's good. I imagine the only thing worse than one sick child is two."

"Pretty much. Though it's just an ear infection, so I don't have to worry about Cassidy catching anything."

"Why's that?"

"Ear infections aren't contagious."

"Oh." A blush crept into her cheeks. "That's good." Smiling, she perched beside Emma. "I brought you some of my granny's famous chicken soup."

"Why is it famous?" Emma cocked her head.

"Well…" Celeste set the basket on the coffee table. "Because it's cured some of my worst ear infections and just about any other illness I've ever had."

"Really?"

"Really. And you *do* want to get better, don't you?"

Emma nodded. "I want soup!" She thrust two fists into the air.

Celeste laughed. "Okay, then." She stood and grabbed the basket. "You watch your show while I give this food to your daddy."

"Will you stay and eat with us?" Emma cocked her head.

"Oh. I…hadn't planned…" Suddenly nervous, Celeste glanced at Gage.

"Pleeeze…" Emma was never above begging.

Hands shoved in his pockets, Gage decided Celeste looked kind of cute when she was nervous.

He shrugged. "It's okay with me."

Under Celeste's influence, Emma not only ate the

chicken soup, but asked for seconds. Now the two of them sat on the couch watching Disney's *Cinderella*, while he polished off his meat loaf and mashed potatoes at the table. God bless Celeste for considering the male appetite.

Emma snuggled against their guest, and Celeste didn't seem to mind. She draped an arm over Emma, her dark brown eyes glued to the TV.

By the time Cinderella's carriage turned back into a pumpkin, Emma had fallen asleep in Celeste's lap. Yet Celeste remained enthralled in the show, absently stroking his daughter's hair.

"I can move her, if you like," he said as the movie ended.

"It's all right. I really don't mind." She shifted slightly and smiled down at his daughter, looking relaxed and comfortable. "That was a cute movie. I've never seen it before."

"Never seen it? I thought all little girls watch princess movies."

"Not if their mother is Hillary Ward-Thompson. I was only allowed to watch movies with strong heroines."

"And princesses aren't strong?"

"No, because they rely on the hero to rescue them."

"And that's bad?"

"According to my mother."

That explained a lot. "So…now that you've seen a princess movie, what do you think?"

She pondered a moment. "I don't think Cinderella was weak at all. Come to think of it, the only thing the prince actually rescued her from was that wretched family of hers. And the mice were pretty cute, too."

"Does that mean you liked it?"

"Most definitely. It made me smile and gave me that contented sigh at the end."

"According to *my* mother, that contented sigh is because the heroine found her happily-ever-after."

"Perhaps. Though happily-ever-afters can come in many different forms."

"Yeah." He felt his daughter's forehead and cheeks before settling into his recliner. "I think her temp's back to normal."

"Her color looks better." Celeste eyed him a moment then looked away. "I'm sorry if I was a little bossy today, when I told you she was sick."

"But you're always bossy."

She shot him a perturbed glance.

"I'm kidding." For the most part, anyway.

"I wasn't questioning your skill as a father. But when Emma said she wanted her daddy, well…it kind of stirred up some sad memories."

"What kind of memories?" he asked as he leaned back in his recliner.

"My dad was always my main caretaker because my mom traveled so much for work. I got sick shortly after they divorced and Granny came to live with us." Her gaze drifted away. "That was the worst sickness ever. All I wanted was my dad. Even Granny's chicken soup didn't fill that void."

"How old were you?"

"Eight."

Just a year older than Cassidy. He wondered about his girls and how the absence of their mother affected them.

Celeste adjusted Emma's blanket. "You're a good father, Gage. Cassidy and Emma are lucky to have you."

"I'd do just about anything for them." He stretched, then leaned forward, resting his forearms on his thighs. "Though I feel like I'm in over my head most of the time."

"Don't be so hard on yourself."

"What? My cooking skills are pretty much limited to fish sticks, mac and cheese and scrambled eggs. I can't tell the difference between Princess Barbie and Ball Gown Barbie, and I can't braid hair to save my life."

Celeste's gentle smile encouraged him. "Maybe. But you love them and you're here for them. That's all they really need."

He knew she was right. But his heart wanted so much more for his daughters. And watching Celeste's tender, nurturing manner only amplified that longing.

"Do you mind if I ask what happened to their mother?"

The question immediately sent him back to that fateful day when he'd come home to find Tracy's bags packed. At least the pain no longer accompanied the memory.

I didn't want one child, let alone two, Gage. This isn't the kind of life I want.

He knew she'd never been keen on the idea of kids, but he thought she'd change her mind. Instead, she sacrificed his daughters at the altar of her dreams.

"Other things became more important to her than motherhood. She said she was tired of waiting for her life to begin." He shrugged. "So she left to start a new one."

"Do the girls ever see her?"

"No. She pretty much cut the cord on that relationship."

Celeste shook her head, her sympathetic gaze falling to Emma.

Then he realized it wasn't sympathy he saw, but empathy. Celeste had suffered the same betrayal of a parent that his girls had. And she understood the extent of their loss better than anyone. Including him.

After a few moments, she sat up. "It's getting late. I should be going."

"Of course." He stood and moved to lift Emma from her lap. The child curled against his chest with a soft sigh.

Celeste stood and tugged on her raincoat. "I'll grab my basket and be out of your hair."

"Let me tuck this little one into bed and I'll see you out."

"No, you take your time. I'll be fine." She went into the kitchen, returning with the basket dangling from one hand.

"I'm sure I speak for Emma, too, when I say thank you for dinner."

She stopped in front of him. Stroked Emma's head, then kissed her cheek. "Sleep well, sweet girl."

When she looked up at him, something flashed between them. And based on her sharp intake of air, Celeste had felt it, too.

What was it about this woman that drove him crazy one moment and conjured up images of hearth and home the next?

Celeste looked away suddenly, breaking the connection. "I need to go."

As he watched her move toward the door, something twisted inside his heart.

And he found himself wishing the night didn't have to end.

Chapter Seven

Celeste wasn't easily shaken. But whatever had passed between her and Gage Saturday night not only sent her scurrying home, the conflicted feelings it triggered had persisted into Sunday and Monday. Lucky for her, Monday's anxiety was soon dulled by exhaustion.

It had taken all day to move everything—from tables and chairs to pots and pans, work tables, dishes and just about anything that wasn't nailed down—from the restaurant into a portable storage pod. Her muscles had never been so sore. She collapsed into bed that night, her mind numb.

When she awoke Tuesday morning, all she could think about was the fact that Granny's Kitchen would be closed at least through the rest of the week. Then she'd be faced with another grueling day when they moved everything back.

Good thing she was meeting with Blakely and Gage today to discuss preparations for the fall festival. Perhaps planning for that would help keep her mind off the restaurant.

Since her body clock woke her up at five thirty, she decided to continue her daily ritual and make a batch of cinnamon rolls. Who knew that making cinnamon rolls had such healing power? Eating them, yes, but making them had never felt so good. Easing the kinks out of her weary muscles. And her condo smelled amazing.

Three pans of rolls were a bit much to carry, though, so she opted to drive to Blakely's house. Besides, with temps hovering in the upper thirties, despite the bright sunshine, the rolls would have been stone-cold by the time she arrived.

Pulling up to the pretty Dutch Colonial, she pondered the rest of her week. This afternoon she planned to become one with her phone and make some real headway on donations and festival volunteers. Beyond that, she didn't have a clue.

She slung the small tote bag holding her notes and iPad tablet over her shoulder and grabbed the still-warm cinnamon rolls from the passenger seat before exiting the vehicle. The fall colors that lined the street were exceptionally beautiful in the morning sun. The vivid gold and orange hues were breathtakingly vibrant.

Her gaze drifted up the mountain, sparking an idea. She should take a drive one day this week. Maybe head down to the old mining town of Ironton. Do a little exploring, take some pictures and enjoy the outdoors for a change.

Gage pulled up behind her then, extinguishing every thought from her brain and sending her heart into a little tap dance.

"Is that what I think it is?" Gage pointed to the foil-covered pans she carried.

"Depends. If you're thinking cinnamon rolls, you'd be correct." Despite her best efforts, she couldn't help smiling.

He took two of the pans as they started up the walk. "Ooh, and they're warm. Even better."

"Since our pregnant friend has been craving them, I thought she'd appreciate it. She can keep them in the freezer and heat them up as she likes."

Gage turned her way, looking suddenly forlorn. "Don't tell me they're *all* for Blakely."

"You're worse than a kid." She climbed the three concrete steps that led to the porch. "But no, one pan is for sharing." She knocked on the door.

Blakely swung the door open. "Hey, guys. Come on in."

"I think Celeste here is vying for Taryn's best-friend spot." Gage gestured toward the pans.

Blakely turned a surprised smile to the other woman. "You brought me cinnamon rolls?"

"The restaurant is going to be closed for a week. I wouldn't want to be responsible for sending you into labor or anything."

"I'm not worried about that, though I might not be fit to live with." Blakely led them across beautiful dark hardwood floors into the spacious kitchen. "You can set them here." She motioned to the granite-topped island, then proceeded to grab plates and forks.

Setting them alongside the pans, Blakely grimaced, reaching for the small of her back. Much the way she had during their meeting last week.

"You okay?" Concern littered Gage's expression.

"Yeah." Blakely smiled again. "These stupid contractions didn't bother me at all this weekend, but they started up again this morning." She pulled the foil from one of the pans and took a plate from the stack. "This should make me feel better, though."

"You have a beautiful home." Celeste took in the adjoining family room, the rustic beams overhead. "Great fireplace." She'd always been a fan of stone fireplaces.

"Thank you." Blakely spoke around a bite of roll.

A few minutes later, they gathered around the kitchen table to go over assignments and progress updates.

Blakely's brow furrowed as she opened her notebook, and Celeste wondered if she was having another one of those pains.

"I scheduled our workday for this Saturday, like we discussed. Gage, if you can have those cutouts ready, we'll have the volunteers paint them."

"I plan to start working on them this afternoon."

"How many volunteers do you have?" Celeste tugged the tablet from her bag and set it on the table.

"For the workday, eight to ten." Blakely turned to Gage. "By the way, Taryn said she should be able to help."

"Oh, so you talked to the newlywed." He grinned.

"She called shortly before you guys got here. She was a little surprised to hear all that transpired in the week that she and Cash were in Belize on their honeymoon, but she's more than happy to volunteer."

"Yeah, I figured we'd be able to count on her." He reached for a third roll. Not that Celeste was counting. "I talked to my friend about the inflatables and we're all set. I'm scheduled to pick them up that Friday before the festival."

"Wonderful."

Celeste folded the cover back on her tablet and called up the spreadsheet she'd assembled. "And I spoke with one of my suppliers. They're willing to donate burgers and hot dogs."

Blakely's jaw dropped. "How on earth did you manage that? The dogs are easy, I know, but we usually end up having to buy the burgers."

"I simply asked."

"That's it?"

"Yes."

"Must have been your gorgeous smile then." Blakely's laugh morphed into a groan.

"Are you sure those contractions are false?" Gage eyed their friend suspiciously. "Because they're coming every six minutes."

"Six minutes?" Panic flitted across Blakely's face. "But I'm not due for another twenty-seven days."

His gaze fell to her swollen belly. "Then I think somebody's planning an early arrival."

A myriad of emotions played across Blakely's face. "I guess I'd better call Trent." She stood and retrieved the phone from the counter. "But if this is real, you know what that means."

Gage sent her an annoyed glance. "That you'd better get to the hospital?"

"No. It means you two are in charge of the festival."

Celeste's cinnamon roll turned to lead in her stomach. She and Gage working together? Alone?

You're a professional. You can do this. After all, you've worked with Martha Zane, aka Cruella de Vil.

Yes, but while Martha, a former coworker, went for the jugular, Gage posed a different kind of threat. One Celeste had never faced before.

An image played across her mind. Emma's excitement when Celeste mentioned the festival Saturday night.

Celeste took a deep breath. She had to do this for the kids. But she'd have to watch every step. Calculate every move. Because if she didn't, her heart was a goner.

And that was a risk she just couldn't take.

In the essence of time, Gage offered to drive Blakely to meet Trent at the clinic in Ridgway. That would put them almost halfway to the hospital and shave off at least twenty minutes had Trent come back to Ouray to pick up his wife. In Gage's experience, second babies were too unpredictable to waste time. He and Tracy had barely made it to the hospital before Emma decided to make her arrival.

Now, as he drove back to Ouray, Celeste sat in the passenger seat, staring out the window. He'd asked her to come with them, just in case something unexpected happened along the way, if not for moral support.

She folded her hands in her lap. "Is autumn always so colorful around here?"

"I suppose." He looked out over the orange-and-gold-dotted rangeland. "I think we've about hit our peak, though."

"In that case—" she glanced his way "—I'm glad the restaurant is closed so I can enjoy it."

He chuckled. "Boy, I never thought I'd hear you say that. Don't you have fall in Texas?" A legitimate question, since some parts of Texas were considered tropical.

"Yes, but it's rare that the colors are so vibrant. Even then, the leaves don't really start falling until around Thanksgiving."

"That's hard to imagine. We're apt to have our first snowfall long before then."

She laughed. "Now *that's* hard for me to imagine." Shifting slightly, she angled toward him. "So it looks like we're in charge of the fall festival."

"Yep." He blew out a breath, not thrilled about the turn of events. Helping was one thing, taking on the whole kit and caboodle was another. Still, he'd hate to see his daughters disappointed.

"You okay with that?" She continued to watch him, the pavement humming beneath the tires of his truck.

"Guess I'll have to be. Besides, God's got a reason for everything, right?"

"That He does."

"Well, I, for one, am glad He knows what He's doing, because I sure don't."

She reached to the floorboard then and pulled out her tablet. "With only two and a half weeks until the festival, I'll admit that I'm more than a little nervous." She lifted the cover and moved her finger around the screen. "According to my calculations, with more than a dozen booths to man over a four-hour period, at two people per one-hour shift, we'll need almost a hundred volunteers. And that's not including setup and teardown."

He darted a glance in his rearview mirror. "You do realize that some people will want to work more than one shift, don't you?"

"Perhaps, but, as of right now, we have zero volunteers."

"That's not true. Blakely said Taryn's willing to help and I know my mom will, too. So we're at two."

"Nonetheless, we're going to have to make some phone calls." She pulled out a sheet of paper, tore it in half and handed one side to him. "Here's a list of potential volunteers. With both of us contacting folks, we can get things done that much faster."

"Oh, no." His grip tightened on the steering wheel. "Don't include me in that. I have cutouts to work on. Besides, I'm not exactly a phone person."

"Gage, those cutouts can wait. Without volunteers, this festival won't happen. That is, unless you plan to man every booth all by yourself." An exaggerated smile accompanied her sarcasm.

Was she trying to press his buttons? So she used to be some big corporate executive. That didn't mean she was always right. "And if I don't get these booths in order, there won't be anything to man." He looked at her now.

"Which reminds me, I think I'll pull into the park when we hit town so we can see about the layout."

She rolled her eyes. "You have got to be—Gage, look out!"

He jerked his gaze forward as a bull elk darted in front of his truck. His foot slammed on the brakes, but it was too late. They were going to hit it.

He yanked the steering wheel to the right. Tires squealed.

They barely missed the animal. But the maneuver sent them careening into the ditch.

The uneven ground thudded beneath them.

Celeste let go a gasp.

Instinctively, he thrust his right arm out to protect her from the impact.

Air whooshed out of both their lungs as the vehicle jolted to a stop.

Celeste's tablet tumbled onto the floor.

For a moment, they sat in stunned silence, only the rumble of the engine and their collective breaths echoing through the pickup's cab.

A groan from Celeste brought him to his senses. He hastily undid his seat belt and leaned across the center console.

"Celeste?" *Lord, please let her be okay.*

Her head lolled toward him, ratcheting his panic up another notch. A moment later, her dazed espresso eyes met his. "Did we hit it?"

He let go a nervous laugh. "No. The elk is fine."

"Good." A lazy smile crossed her lips. She straightened, hissing in a breath.

"What is it? Are you hurt?" Heart pounding, he did a quick visual. What if she was injured? The impact could have broken a bone.

"Stupid seat belt." Reaching one hand to her neck, she used the other to unhook her belt.

"Let me see."

She twisted enough for him to glimpse the raw, red area on the right side of her neck.

He winced. "Yeah, that seat belt didn't do you any favors."

"Except keep me from flying through the windshield."

He smiled. "I suppose there is that."

He carefully brushed her silky hair out of the way, tucking it behind her ear. She'd worn it down today, the golden waves spilling over her shoulders. Something he could get used to. Along with the jeans and cowboy boots. This was only the second time he'd seen her in anything other than business attire, the first being yesterday when they'd emptied the restaurant. He had to give Celeste credit. She was a hard worker. And, despite his earlier beliefs, she wasn't afraid to get dirty.

He forced himself to look at the wound.

"It's not bleeding." His fingers grazed the back of her neck. Her skin was as soft as a rose petal. "But it's probably going to sting for a while."

She nodded. "Um…what about you? Are you okay?" Her gaze flitted to his.

"I think so. Though, I think we'll both have a stiff neck tomorrow." He knew he should move away, give her some space. Instead, he wanted to pull her into his arms and show her how glad he was that she was all right.

Someone pounded on the driver's side window just then, startling both him and Celeste.

"You folks okay in there?"

Gage turned around to find a man and woman staring at them. Talk about awkward. He felt like a teenager who just got caught parking with his girlfriend.

He pushed the button to roll down the window, allowing cool air to filter into the cab. "Yeah. We're fine."

"That sure was an impressive elk." The man looked to be around seventy.

Gage eyed the Oklahoma license plate on the RV parked behind him. "I'm afraid I didn't get that good a look at him."

The man grinned. "No, I don't s'pose you did." He eyed Celeste.

"We just wanted to make sure y'all weren't hurt." His wife's face pressed closer to the window.

"Bless your hearts. Y'all are so sweet." Since when had Celeste turned into a Southern belle?

"Well, it's just the right neighborly thing to do," said the woman.

"Yes, ma'am."

He dared a look and sure enough, Celeste was batting her eyes. Was she having fun with these people or genuinely appreciative? Not that he didn't appreciate the couple checking on them. Bad things happened because too many people failed to get involved these days.

"Come on, Marvadeen. We best be letting these two git on their way." The man moved away from the truck.

"Bye, y'all." The woman waved.

The moment Gage rolled up his window, he and Celeste burst out laughing.

"Gotta love it," he said.

"Aw, they were cute, Gage."

"I don't know about cute, but they were *right neighborly*."

"Stop." She playfully swatted his arm.

"You ready to head on back to town there, missy?" He applied his best Southern drawl. "Because I do believe we have some phone calls to make."

Chapter Eight

Celeste parked her Mustang convertible across from Granny's Kitchen Friday morning. Setting her boot-clad feet on the gravel, she exited and eyed the restaurant. Large dryer-type hoses were still attached to the upstairs windows, snaking their way to special industrial-sized HEPA filters, and plastic sheeting seemed to be everywhere.

The fact that she couldn't go inside to see what was happening did not set well. She could only pray that they'd be done soon.

The sound of crunching gravel snagged her attention as Gage whipped his truck into the spot beside her. She'd successfully managed to avoid him since Wednesday, though the memories of their close encounter remained. The caring look in his deep blue eyes. The way he smelled, like soap and cinnamon.

Then he'd spent the rest of the afternoon helping her make phone calls. By the time he'd left to pick up the girls, they had at least one person to cover every booth on every shift.

She shook the memories away as he got out of his truck.

"What are you doing here?"

"Same as you." She folded her arms across her chest to ward against the morning chill. "Checking to see how things are going."

"And?"

"I don't know. I just got here."

His smile reached past her walls into her heart and shook out the kinks. "Let's go find out then."

The project manager was on his cell phone but waved as they approached. "They're right here, so I'll let them know." He ended the call and clipped the phone to the holder on his belt. "Good news. Our job is done."

"Excellent." Gage's smile mirrored her own.

"That was the inspector on the phone." The manager continued. "He'll be out late this afternoon to take an air sample. With any luck, you'll have your results early next week and be back in business."

Celeste wanted to jump for joy. "I can't tell you how happy this makes me. Thank you for getting this done so quickly."

Walking away, she felt as though a weight had been lifted from her shoulders. She turned to Gage. "This calls for a celebration. Have you had breakfast?"

"No. But I'm headed to meet some friends." He shoved his hands into the pockets of his jeans. "You're welcome to join us."

Her insides cringed. What had she been thinking? Inviting Gage to breakfast when she was trying to avoid him? Obviously, her emotions had gotten the best of her. "No, I don't think so. It wouldn't be right for me to impose on your friends."

"You're not imposing. Matter of fact, there's something I'd like to show you."

Squinting against the sun's rays as they broke over the Amphitheater, she said, "What about your friends?"

"Are you kidding? They'll love having a pretty girl in their midst."

Her heart tripped. Gage thought she was pretty?

"And they rustle up a pretty mean breakfast. No cinnamon rolls, just some tasty bacon and eggs."

The thought of bacon made her stomach growl. She dragged the toe of her boot through the dirt, curious as to what Gage wanted to show her.

"Well, if you're sure they won't mind."

"Positive." He motioned to his truck. "Okay if I drive? I'm not sure how well your car would do on the mountain roads."

Mountain roads? Where was he taking her?

Her gaze narrowed. "So long as you promise *not* to get distracted."

His sheepish grin reminded her of Cassidy. "I promise."

He kept his eyes on the road as they headed north on Main Street.

She, on the other hand, reveled in the opportunity to take in the scenery. "What's that statue by the hot springs?"

"That's the Miner's Memorial," he said as they passed.

She twisted for a better look. "I guess I've never really paid attention to it before."

He maneuvered the next curve, the corners of his mouth lifting into a boyish smile. "Have I ever told you I'm a miner by trade?"

"I don't believe so. Then why are you doing construction?" Though, if it were her, she'd take construction over working in some cold, dark space.

"Because the mines aren't hiring right now." He shrugged. "At least not someone with my qualifications."

She had to admit, her knowledge of mining was limited to the gold rush-era stuff her grandfather used to tell her.

"Are you saying you're overqualified?"

"Kind of. I'm a mining engineer." He sent her a quick glance. "Same basic knowledge as most engineers, only my area of expertise is mines. Design, safety, sustainability."

"Hmm. And here I thought miners just marched into a dark tunnel with their hard hats and a candle and set off explosions."

He laughed. "Long ago, maybe. People don't realize that there's a high demand for vital minerals from the earth. Much more than just gold and silver. In this day and age, we need to be able to extract those minerals as safely and efficiently as we can. That's where I come in."

"Interesting. So what made you decide to go into mining?"

"Well, for starters, I grew up in Ouray. This place is surrounded with mines." He waved a hand around him. "All those tales of striking it rich intrigued me." He grinned. "Mom used to worry every time I went exploring. She was afraid I'd fall in or something."

"Can't say I blame her."

He veered onto a county road just north of town. "I used to work for the Amrada mine outside of Denver." The truck bumped up the gravel road. "It was my dream job. But after Tracy left…" He raked a hand through his hair. "I couldn't give Cassidy and Emma the attention they deserved. So we came back to Ouray to be near my family."

A boulder-size lump caught in her throat. Cassidy and

Emma's mother had left to follow her dreams. Yet Gage sacrificed his for his daughters.

Celeste swallowed the emotion that had momentarily rendered her speechless. "You are a man of great character, Gage."

He chortled. "Why do you say that?"

"You gave up your dreams for Cassidy and Emma. God will honor that."

"He already has. He continues to provide me with a steady income. Though I do wish He'd open some doors for me at one of the mines around here."

"He will. In His time."

The road grew steeper and he shifted into a lower gear.

"Anyway—" he sent her a quick glance "—what I was going to tell you is that we're going to a mine."

"A mine?" She straightened, her insides suddenly churning.

"Not a working mine. One they use for tours."

"Bachelor-Syracuse, right?"

"Have you been up here?"

"No. But I've heard a lot of my customers talk about it."

"Celeste, you really need to get out of the restaurant more often. Start doing some things, instead of just hearing about them."

"I'm beginning to realize that." Though going into a dark mine wasn't exactly at the top of her list. "I went down to Ironton yesterday and just wandered around those old buildings. Very peaceful. Got some great pictures, too. I think I might have a couple blown up to hang in the restaurant."

After a quick right turn, Gage parked his truck between a Jeep SUV and a 4x4 pickup.

As soon as Celeste hopped out, the aroma of fresh-cooked bacon reached her nose, rekindling her appetite.

Gage led her past a small building with an old ore car parked in front that read Ticket Office. A little farther down, a cluster of picnic tables were grouped in front of a stainless steel counter. At one of the tables, four men nursed foam cups of what she assumed was coffee.

"Gage." A man close to his age stood. "Good to see you, buddy."

The two shook hands.

"You, too." Gage touched Celeste's shoulder. "Ted, this is Celeste Thompson. She's the owner of Granny's Kitchen."

"I thought you looked familiar." Ted's hand swung in her direction. "Ted Beatty, nice to meet you."

Gage introduced her to the other three men before urging her toward the counter.

"Hey there, Gage." An older fellow with a peppering of gray in his otherwise dark brown hair smiled from his post at a commercial-size outdoor griddle where eggs bubbled and bacon sizzled. "Glad you could make it."

"Celeste, this is Clay Musgrove. He runs things up here."

"Pleasure to meet you, Clay. Your breakfast smells wonderful."

He smiled. "Then I hope you'll consider joining a bunch of crusty old codgers."

"I don't know where you have them hidden, but I would love to."

Clay eyed Gage. "She ought to fit right in."

"Speaking of fitting in, would you mind if I took her in the mine?"

Take her in the mine? Her muscles tightened as the nausea returned with a vengeance.

"Go right ahead. You know where the helmets and the jackets are."

Gage headed around the back of the ticket office.

She followed, albeit with a good bit of hesitation. "Wait. You're taking me *into* the mine?"

"Yep." He continued into an open area at the back of the building.

Despite the cool morning air, Celeste began to sweat. Her heart raced. She'd never been a fan of caves or caverns of any kind. She didn't even like it when she got caught under an overpass in her car. All she could think about was what if there was an earthquake or a cave-in. She'd be buried alive. And Gage expected her to go through some long dark tunnel into the belly of a mountain?

The thought stopped her in her tracks, her feet firmly planted in the pea gravel.

"I'm sorry, Gage. I can't do this." Turning on her heel, she headed back to his truck.

Disappointment wound its way into Gage's spirit, putting him in a foul mood that spilled into Saturday. To make matters worse, he couldn't even justify it. He'd seen the fear in Celeste's eyes yesterday. Felt the trembling of her hands. Her unwillingness to go into the mine had nothing to do with him. Yet, somehow, he'd managed to make it all about him.

Why had he felt so compelled to share his love of mining with her anyway?

He was an idiot. Hadn't he vowed never to marry again? Not to let his heart get tangled in the trappings of love. Not only to protect himself, but his daughters. But ever since they ran off the road Wednesday, Celeste seemed to have taken up residence in his brain, not to mention his heart. He kept thinking about the softness of her skin, her beautiful hair. The strength, yet vulnerability, in her dark gaze. And the overwhelming urge he had to protect her.

Maybe he had hit his head. Hard.

Shoving his frustration aside, he drove his truck up Second Street in the direction of Restoration Fellowship. He needed to focus on the festival, not Celeste. At least a dozen volunteers would be arriving at the church soon and it was his job to make sure they stayed busy.

"Cassidy stickeded her tongue out at me."

"Nuh-uh. I was just licking the peanut butter off of my lip."

Back to reality.

"Girls." He eyed them in the backseat via the rearview mirror. "You promised you'd behave today." Reaching a hand behind him, he patted Emma's knee. "Try giving your sister the benefit of the doubt, okay?"

"Okay." She turned toward Cassidy. "Next time you should point your tongue someplace else, cuz it lookeded like you were sticking it out at me."

Gage shook his head, grateful that his mother would also be at the church. He'd need all the help he could get.

Don't forget about Celeste.

Groaning, he swung into a parking space. Best he could do was stay focused, get the job done and make sure he and the girls interacted with Celeste as little as possible.

While the girls hopped out, he unloaded the cutouts from the bed of his truck. Thanks to his wayward thoughts, they weren't quite finished. Holes for the suckers still needed to be drilled in the lollipop tree, but he could do that after they were painted.

"Oh, good, you're here." Celeste appeared at the side entrance of the church, her tablet in hand.

"Celeste!" The girls cheered and ran to greet her.

She smiled when she saw them, her open arms awaiting hugs.

"Girls." He wished they wouldn't do that. So much for limited interaction.

"It's all right, Gage. I don't mind." She embraced each of his daughters. "One can never get too many hugs, right, girls?"

The whole trio giggled.

He tossed the lollipop tree onto the grass.

"Can we help you?" Cassidy beamed at Celeste.

"Of course, you—"

"I was counting on the girls to help me." He grabbed the cutout for the football toss and set it beside the lollipop tree as Emma started toward him.

"Do we get to paint?"

Uh-oh. His knee-jerk reaction was about to get him into trouble. His goal had been to keep them away from Celeste. But what could he have them do?

"Not this time. But you can help me clean up the games we're reusing. Like the ring toss, the fishing game…"

Emma's face reddened, her bottom lip growing bigger by the second. "I don't wanna clean. I wanna help Celeste." Her arms crossed over her chest.

Oh, no. And here he thought she was doing better.

"I'll let you do the squirt bottle," he said.

"No!" Her response was accentuated by an all-too-familiar foot stomp.

Lord, a little help here.

Out of the corner of his eye, he saw Celeste set her tablet inside and start toward them. Interfering again, just like she had at Taryn's wedding.

"Ooh, can I do the squirt bottle?" Smiling, she slipped both hands into the back pockets of her faded jeans.

Birds chirped overhead as he stood there dumbfounded.

You asked for help.

"I like to clean. And on a beautiful day like this—" she gestured to the cloudless sky "—I'd much rather be outside than dealing with some dusty old stuff that's been packed away for a year."

Play along, stupid.

"All right, then. Looks like Celeste gets to do the squirt bottle."

"I never get to do anything fun." Emma stomped again. He couldn't win for losing.

Celeste knelt beside her. "Do you think you can do a good job?"

The child nodded emphatically, her frown dissipating. "Daddy says I'm a good cleaner."

Standing, Celeste eyed him. "I guess it's your call, Dad."

He rubbed his chin. "I don't know."

"Please, Daddy?" Emma bounced beside him. "I promise I'll do good."

Once again, Celeste had managed to thwart another of Emma's tantrums. Leaving him feeling like a heel. What would it have hurt for them to help Celeste?

Now it was up to him to find things to keep the girls occupied. And happy.

Gravel crunched behind him and he turned to see his mother pulling up in her SUV.

Wearing a knowing grin, she got out and closed the door behind her. "My goodness, but you all are a lovely sight."

Oh, brother. Gage had a pretty good idea that the

"sight" she was referring to was all of them—him, Celeste, Cassidy and Emma—together. As in, a family.

Mom was determined to see each of her children enjoying the same life of wedded bliss that she and his father had shared for over thirty-five years. Now that Taryn had married, it was his turn at the plate. Except he had no interest in being on the team.

"Did you bring the spray paint?" Rather than feed his mother's fantasies, he found it best to ignore them.

Her smile unfaltering, she narrowed her gaze in a way that was virtually imperceptible to anyone outside their immediate family. A look that let him know, in no uncertain terms, that they would discuss this later.

"Of course I did. They don't call me the queen of spray paint for nothing."

He followed her to the back of her vehicle, while Celeste chatted with the girls. "Mom." He kept his voice low. "Let it go. I told you, I have no interest in dating, let alone marrying again."

"Yes, you did." She lifted the hatch. "However, I also know how much you want Cassidy and Emma to have a mother. They can't have a mother if you don't have a wife."

Tempering his annoyance, he reached for the cardboard box full of spray cans with colorful caps. He wouldn't be rude to his mother, but this conversation needed to stop. Now. "I have no plans to marry and that's that, Mom."

"Gage, honey—" Her expression softened. A smile replaced her frown, her focus somewhere in the direction of the church. "Many are the plans in a man's heart, but it's the Lord's purpose that prevails."

"What?" Following her gaze, he saw Celeste and the

girls sitting cross-legged in the grass, Cassidy in front of her, Emma beside her.

His throat tightened.

Celeste was braiding Cassidy's hair. And whatever they were talking about had all of them giggling.

Warmth settled into the pit of his stomach. This was what he wanted for his girls. What they deserved.

He forced himself to look away. Unfortunately, life didn't come with a guarantee. His daughters already had their hearts ripped out once. It was only by the grace of God they'd bounced back as well as they had. So to risk their tender hearts again?

That was something he just couldn't do.

Chapter Nine

Celeste fired up her Mustang and pulled away from Blakely's house, trying to remember the last time she'd had a Sunday to herself. She loved Granny's Kitchen with every fiber of her being, but the fact that she didn't have to worry about the restaurant made this day a real treat. She'd even slept until seven o'clock. Which, considering the work that lay ahead this week getting the restaurant put back together, was probably a good thing.

After a leisurely breakfast on her deck overlooking the Uncompahgre River, she'd attended both Sunday school *and* worship service. Something she hadn't done in the six months she'd been in Ouray. She'd gone to worship a few times, but that was it. Still, she knew many of the members from the restaurant and tried to stay as plugged in as possible.

Yet, somewhere along the way, she'd missed the fact that Gage and his daughters also worshipped at Restoration Fellowship. Had she known, though, she might not have been so eager to make it to church this morning. Gage had been acting weird ever since she refused to go in the mine with him. Not mad necessarily, just aloof.

Once the volunteers arrived yesterday, she hardly saw him at all. And this morning, he barely said hello.

Isn't that what you wanted?

Yes.

No.

Maybe.

Letting go a sigh, she maneuvered her car around the corner. To say she was conflicted about Gage would be an understatement. Something strange happened to her every time she was with him. He made her stomach twist into knots. No other man had ever had that kind of effect on her. But, with Gage, her heart was vulnerable and he threatened every belief her mother had instilled in her.

If she were here, she would tell Celeste this was precisely why she didn't need a man in her life. *They only mess with our heads and keep us from thinking clearly.*

But Celeste liked Gage. Not to mention his daughters. And while Celeste definitely didn't need a man to take care of her, Gage ignited thoughts of family and forever.

Visiting Blakely hadn't helped quell those notions, either. When Celeste offered to bring the family lunch today, she hadn't expected her friend to be so eager to deposit their newborn daughter into her arms. Celeste had never held a baby before, let alone one that small.

Weighing in at five pounds ten ounces, Katelynn was the tiniest thing Celeste had ever laid eyes on. And the way she smelled…Celeste breathed deep, recalling the fragrance. So sweet. Blissful. Pure.

By the time all was said and done, she'd ended up staying way longer than she intended, opting to hold the baby while Trent, Blakely and Austin enjoyed their meal. Who knew that something as simple as holding a baby could bring such joy?

She shook her head, grateful she'd elected to put the

top down on her convertible today. The crisp autumn breeze blew through her hair, exhilarating her senses. With any luck, it would carry away the crazy thoughts she'd been entertaining. Thoughts of motherhood, of Gage and Cassidy and Emma.

The midafternoon sun was warm on her skin when she paused at a stop sign. And though she had things to do at home, it was too nice of a day to retreat just yet. Instead, she took a left onto Main Street and followed the winding turns south of town until she came to the overlook.

Exiting her vehicle, she marveled in the majestic view. No matter which way she turned, she was surrounded by mountains. Fir trees meandered up the oft-steep slopes, eventually giving way to barren rock formations. Snow-tipped peaks gleamed under a cloudless sky. A sky that was the bluest blue she'd ever seen.

Gage was right. She really did need to get out of the restaurant more often. One couldn't simply live in Ouray. One needed to experience it.

Pulling out her camera, she snapped one shot after another.

God, if this is not proof of You and Your awesomeness, I don't know what is.

She peered over the top of the camera. Simply breath-taking.

As much as she wanted to linger, there were things she needed to tend to back at her condo. Things like preparing for the reopening of Granny's Kitchen and going over her lists for the fall festival. They'd made a lot of headway yesterday, but she didn't want anything falling through the cracks.

She wound her way back into town and headed straight home. Turning onto Second Street, she noticed two little blond-haired girls chasing each other in the yard across from hers. She smiled, glancing at the beaded bracelets on her wrist. While doing inventory yesterday, someone came across a large bag of beads and some stretchy plastic cord. So, when Cassidy and Emma got bored, Celeste presented them with the find and told them to have fun.

Later, they each gave her a colorful bracelet, stating that they made them especially for Celeste. It was all she could do to hold back tears. No gift had ever meant more.

Thumbing the button on the garage door opener, she waved before turning into her driveway. The girls returned the gesture with a gusto that warmed her heart.

Once safely in the garage, she killed the engine and got out, bringing with her the basket she'd used to take the food to Blakely's.

"What's in the basket?"

She jumped at the sound of Emma's voice. "Sweet girl, you nearly scared me half to death." Moving in the direction of the open door, she noticed that Cassidy was with Emma, but saw no signs of Gage. "Does your father know you two are over here?"

The girls looked at each other before shaking their heads.

"But we wanted to see you," said Emma.

Celeste laid a hand on her shoulder. "I like it when I get to see you, too. But what about your daddy? Don't you think he'd be worried if he came outside and couldn't find you?"

"Yes, ma'am." Cassidy lowered her gaze.

Emma, on the other hand, didn't appear to share her sister's remorse.

"Come on." Celeste set the basket on her trunk then took each girl by the hand and started across the street.

"You didn't tell us what was in the basket." Emma squinted against the sun as she peered up at Celeste.

"Nothing. I used it to take some food to a friend."

"What kind of food?" Emma was nothing if not curious.

"Oh, some pot roast, mashed potatoes, green beans… and some cookies."

"Cookies? I love cookies."

"Celeste already said the basket was empty." Cassidy glowered at her sister.

But I have more at home. Celeste had to keep from blurting the words out. As much as she'd love to have the girls come to her house, Gage might have other plans.

About the time they reached the bottom step, Gage emerged from his house. "Girls— Oh, there you are." He smiled down at them. That is, until his gaze landed on Celeste.

Emma let go of her hand and marched up the steps. "We wanted to see Celeste, Daddy."

"They saw me pulling into my driveway," she offered.

"Can we go to Celeste's house? *Please*, Daddy?"

He crossed his arms over his chest in that hulking manner and eyed Emma first, then Celeste. "I'm sure Celeste has better things to do than entertain you two."

Was he trying to spare her or did he actually believe she'd be bothered by his daughters? True, she did have things to do, but nothing that couldn't wait. She slept late, after all. Meaning she'd likely be up late.

"I don't mind." She sent him her best smile, hoping to erase that wary expression of his. "Matter of fact, you're welcome to come, too, if you like." As soon as the words left her mouth, she wanted to take them back. She wanted to spend time with Cassidy and Emma. Having Gage there might change the dynamics. Or at least make her behave like somebody other than herself.

Cassidy released her other hand, then bounded up the stairs. "Oh, yes, Daddy. Please say you'll come, too."

Over the next few moments, Gage refused to look at either her or the girls. He shifted his weight from one foot to the next. His jaw flexed. He didn't want to come. But he also didn't like to disappoint his girls. Still, they'd only be across the street.

"I have some fresh cookies." Stomach fluttering, she wondered why on earth she'd said that.

"Cookies!" Emma bounced alongside her father.

Gage's shoulders drooped. His arms fell to his sides in defeat. "All right, we can go." His gaze sought out Celeste's, emphatic and challenging at the same time. "But just a quick visit."

Somehow she doubted that. *Lord, what have I gotten myself into?*

Gage could think of at least a dozen other things he'd rather be doing besides hanging out in Celeste's pristine condo. He was missing the Broncos game, for crying out loud. Midway through the third quarter they were behind, but only by a field goal.

His girls wanted to be here, though. And given his mixed emotions regarding Celeste, that meant he needed to be here, too.

Topping the stairs that led to the condo's main living area, he was surprised to see boxes of pantry items and pans stacked along the wall in the dining room, the table covered in stacks of papers and the glass-topped coffee table still bearing signs of last night's dinner. Not nearly as fussy as he remembered.

"You'll have to excuse the mess." Celeste dropped the basket and her purse into a chair and hurried to retrieve the plate and cup from the living room. "I got a little lazy this week." Pink tinged her cheeks as she scurried into the kitchen, as though she were nervous or embarrassed. Both out of character.

Suddenly feeling the need to put her at ease, he said, "No problem. I mean, it's not like I'm known for my spotless house."

Returning, she sent him a shy smile. Something he hadn't seen before. And found annoyingly attractive.

"Ooh...pretty cups," said Emma.

Grateful for the distraction, he searched for his daughters, finding them on the other side of the room, their noses pressed against the glass of a curio cabinet. Funny, he thought they were right beside him.

"Aren't they, though?" Celeste moved toward them. "That's my Granny's teacup collection." She twisted a switch on the cord behind the case, illuminating the colorful display. "Which one do you like the best?"

"I like the one with the pink flowers." Emma was as animated as ever.

"I think that one is my favorite." Cassidy pointed to a deep purple cup with gold trim.

When it came to colors, his girls were so predictable.

"Excellent choice," said Celeste.

"Which one is your favorite?" Cassidy waited.

"Hmm..." Celeste furrowed her brow. "That's a hard choice, because I like them all. But if I had to choose just one—" she opened the case and reached inside "—it would have to be this one." She picked up a cream-colored cup with blue flowers trailing up the side.

"I like that one, too," said Emma.

Celeste laughed. "Say, do you girls like milk with your cookies?"

Both nodded.

"Me, too. So what do you say we drink our milk from our favorite teacup?"

"Yay!" Emma bounced.

"Whoa. Hey." Touching Celeste's elbow, Gage tried to ignore the softness of her sweater and tugged her aside. "Are you sure you want to do that? After all, they were your grandmother's." He glanced at his daughters. "What if they broke one?"

She looked up at him with those dark eyes. "Gage, my grandmother always said that beautiful things were meant to be enjoyed. She used to let me drink from them when I was their age. I think she would be delighted to see your girls enjoying them, too."

That sounded like Mrs. Ward. He remembered her letting him play with some of the old mining gear at her restaurant. "If you're sure."

"I am." She turned back to the girls. "Which one do you think your daddy would like?" She cocked her head in his direction, a glint of sass sparking in her gaze. "Or would you prefer a manly mug, perhaps in front of the football game?"

"Now you're speaking my language."

She glanced at the pendulum clock on the wall. "The Cowboys game doesn't start for another forty-five minutes, but I'm sure there's another game till then."

"Cowboys? Who gives a hoot about them? Broncos are probably in the fourth quarter by now."

She set the cup on the table, thrust her hands onto her hips and strode toward him until they were high-heeled toe-to-booted toe. Which meant the top of her head still fell somewhere below his chin.

Her gaze narrowed as she looked up. "I give a hoot about them. The Cowboys are *my* team and this is *my* house. So if you don't like it, you can take *your* cookies elsewhere."

Mimicking her stance, he peered down at her. "You expect me to believe you actually like football?"

Her brow lifted. "Season ticket holder for the past five years."

Why did she have to blow every preconceived notion he had about her out of the water?

Realizing he was digging his own grave, he lifted his hands in surrender and backed away. "Touché."

After sending him a satisfied grin, she moved past him and turned on the television. "Though I have no doubt my granny would approve of my loyalties, she'd frown upon me treating a guest badly. So, in the spirit of hospitality—" she changed the channel to the Broncos game "—I will allow you to finish your game." Returning to the dining room, she shoved the remote into his hand as she passed.

Note to self: do not dis the Dallas Cowboys in Celeste's presence.

He settled onto the leather sofa while Celeste and the girls cleared off a spot at the table. A short time later, the girls appeared at his side.

"Here you go, Daddy." Emma handed him a plate of cookies.

Cassidy held out a thick white mug filled with milk.

"Why, thank you, ladies." He caught Celeste's eye across the room. "A guy could get used to this, you know."

"You just watch your game. We girls have work to do."

"What work?"

She shooed him with her hand. "Mind your own business."

Fine by him.

Savoring both the cookies and the game, he found

himself relaxing. Occasionally, the giggles and chatter of two little girls drowned out the play calls and cheers from the TV. But he knew they were having fun.

A short time later, a strong, distinctive odor wafted over to the living room.

He looked into the dining room. With the cookies gone, they'd moved on to painting their fingernails.

That would never happen at his house. He rarely thought about all those girlie things his daughters liked so much. Listening to their happy voices, though, he couldn't help thinking that this was how things were supposed to be. A dad. A mom. Each with different strengths.

The thought echoed in his mind as his beloved Broncos kicked the game-winning field goal. In some ways, Celeste was so much like Tracy. Yet in others, they were worlds apart. He flipped the channel to Celeste's game.

"Look at our nails, Daddy." Emma wiggled her small fingers in front of him. As did her sister. Silver and blue alternated on each nail.

"Aw, come on, Celeste…really?"

Wearing a satisfied grin, she plunked down in the chair, kicked off her heels and revealed her own dual-color nails. "Just getting into the spirit of the game."

A few minutes in and the Cowboys were first and goal.

"Come on, Cowboys!" Celeste's voice held a gravelly tone.

"'Mon, Cowboys!" Emma mimicked their hostess.

He cast his daughter a curious look. "I thought you didn't like football."

"I don't. I just like cowboys."

She liked horses, too, but— "Sweetheart, do you see any cowboys out there?" He nodded toward the TV.

"Uh-huh."

"Where?"

"Right there." She pointed just as the camera got a shot of the team's mascot. "Isn't he cute, Daddy?"

He couldn't win for losing today.

By halftime, Gage was a little more into the game. After all, since the Broncos were in a completely different conference, he could enjoy the game without caring who won or lost.

As the sun dipped below the mountains, bathing the town in shadows, he stood, knowing that he should think about getting the girls home.

Celeste whisked past him and he caught a whiff of vanilla as she reached to turn on a lamp. The incandescent light filled the room with a warm glow.

Looking around, he decided that her place wasn't nearly as stuffy as he'd thought that night he'd come to help with the bear. Instead, he found it inviting.

"What's out there?" Emma pointed to the French doors on the far dining room wall.

"That's my deck." Celeste opened the door and they all went outside.

"Great view." Hands clasped, he rested his forearms on the railing and listened to the low rumble of the river. During the late spring and early summer, when the snowmelt was at its peak, the sound of the Uncompahgre could be almost deafening.

"Look, Daddy. A table." Emma hopped into one of the two iron chairs beside the small round table that had been tucked in one corner.

"Sure enough." He again focused on the view as Celeste came alongside him. "You sit out here much?"

She shrugged. "Considering I spend most of my time at the restaurant, not so much. But I did have breakfast out here this morning." She pointed upstream. "Saw a really nice buck down there, too." She was quiet for a moment, her gaze fixed somewhere across the river. "I've got some pot roast and mashed potatoes, if you all would like to stay for dinner."

As much as he hated to admit it, he was enjoying himself. Way more than he should. And the girls did need to eat. Something more than the macaroni and cheese he had planned.

"Sounds great." He turned to find her looking at him. "That is, if you don't mind."

"I wouldn't have offered if I did."

He couldn't help smiling. "Well, then. Okay."

While Celeste recruited the girls to help with the preparations, Gage watched from the dining room. What would it be like to come home to a woman like Celeste? Dinner on the table. Spending time together as a family?

He shook his head. Crazy. Celeste was no different than Tracy. More nurturing, perhaps. Not to mention a great cook. But she was a businesswoman at heart. What if she decided Ouray wasn't where she belonged? That she'd made a mistake leaving Texas and her high-powered job?

Many are the plans in a man's heart...

His mother's—and God's—words played through his mind.

Lord, You know my plans to never marry again. But do You have a different purpose?

If so, the Lord was going to have to make it perfectly clear. Because Gage did not want to see his daughters hurt again.

Then what are you doing here now?

The doorbell rang then, disrupting his thoughts.

"Would you mind getting that for me?" Celeste barely looked his way, her attention focused on the girls and a pot of potatoes.

"No problem." He jogged down the stairs, curious who might be paying Celeste a visit. Then again, she knew most everyone in town from the restaurant. Maybe someone wanted to know when Granny's Kitchen would be open again. Or maybe it was Trent in need of some cinnamon rolls for Blakely.

He flipped the switch on the porch light and pulled open the door.

A woman close to his mother's age stood on the other side, looking surprised. "I'm sorry." Taking a step back, she appeared to double-check the house number. "I thought this was Celeste Thompson's condo."

"It is." He leaned against the door. "May I tell her who's calling?" Too late, he noticed the short blond hair and perfectly tailored blazer over a crisp button-down shirt. And her narrowed gaze told him she was not happy.

"Hillary Ward-Thompson. Her mother."

Chapter Ten

Celeste waved good-night to Gage and the girls and closed the front door. Leaning against it, she took a deep breath. To say she was blindsided by her mother's visit would be the understatement of the century. Her mother was a master planner. Even the smallest details were plugged into her day planner, with no room for deviation. So Celeste wasn't buying that her mother "simply wanted to see her." Hillary didn't do anything without a reason.

Upstairs in the kitchen, she found her mother at the coffeepot, pouring her third cup in less than two hours. While Celeste was a one-cup-in-the-morning kind of girl, her mother would, no doubt, have the poor little four-cup drip machine running from sunup to sundown. It was a good part of the reason her mother was able to maintain her trim figure, because the plain black brew also substituted for many a meal.

"Everyone get off all right?"

"Yes." Celeste snagged the empty mashed potato bowl from the dining table as she passed and continued on to the sink.

"Cute kids." Mom leaned her backside against the counter.

"Aren't they?" Celeste turned on the water. "I love spending time with them."

"I have to say—" her mother cocked her head "—when I decided to visit my daughter, I never expected I'd find such a cozy little scene."

Was that a hint of sarcasm in her mother's voice or simply annoyance? Either way, she needed to douse her mother's suspicions.

Celeste rinsed another plate and set it in the dishwasher. "I adore Cassidy and Emma. And their father likes them to have female role models." She looked at her mother now. "But Gage and I are friends. Nothing more." Regardless of the feelings he seemed to stir inside her every time they were together.

"Well, that's good." Mom strolled around the peninsula, set her cup on the eat-at counter and pulled herself into one of the counter-height chairs. "Because since you've decided to give up everything you've ever worked for and pour your heart and soul into that restaurant, there's no room in your life for a man."

This time her mother's sarcasm was impossible to miss.

"How long has the restaurant been closed?" Mom peered over the rim of her mug as she took a sip.

"Since Monday." Celeste tucked the last plate into the dishwasher, then rinsed the silverware. "I was pleased with how quickly they were able to get the job done. Lord willing, by the end of tomorrow, we'll have the all-clear and I can focus on reopening."

"It's *never* good when a business has to close its doors."

Celeste shoved her annoyance aside. "Oh, I don't know. It's been kind of nice having a few days to myself."

"You've lost a week's worth of income."

"I can handle it, Mom." She closed the dishwasher and

dried her hands on a dish towel, eager to get to the bottom of things. "So, why are you *really* in Ouray?"

"Darling, you're my daughter." Cup in hand, her mother eased out of the chair and moved into the living room. "I've missed you."

Celeste followed. She could wipe down the counters later. "You could have let me know you were coming."

"And ruin the surprise?" Mom perched on the overstuffed chair, looking somewhere between indignant and feigned innocence.

"You hate surprises." Celeste settled on the sofa, grabbed the sage green throw pillow beside her and pulled it into her lap.

Her mother's dark eyes narrowed. "Why am I getting the feeling you don't want me here?"

Avoiding the question. Classic Hillary. Leaving no doubt that her mother had ulterior motives. And Celeste was certain it had to do with her decision to move to Ouray.

"Don't be silly. I'm thrilled that you're here." Or at least stunned. "After all, I've been trying to get you to come visit for the last six months. I only wish I'd had time to prepare."

Mom lifted her cup for another drink, then paused. "I have to say, you look much better than I expected."

"What did you expect?"

"Oh, I don't know. Dark circles. Pale skin." She took a sip. "Your color is actually quite lovely. You must tell me what product you're using to achieve that natural glow."

"Um…the sun." She fiddled with the pillow's fringe. "Since I didn't have to go into the restaurant this week, I was able to spend some time in the mountains and enjoy the outdoors."

"Hmm." Cradling her mug, her mother pretended to take in every nuance of the room.

"Ouray is an amazing place, Mom. I love my job, the people. It feels amazing to be part of a community."

"You're trying too hard, darling."

"What?"

Standing, her mother set her cup on the coffee table and joined Celeste on the sofa. "Singing the praises of Ouray. I don't know who you're trying to convince more, me or yourself."

"Why would I—"

"Celeste, darling, I know it stings to be passed over for a promotion." Her mother took hold of her hand. "But that doesn't mean we give up. We simply try harder for the next one."

"Promotion?" She never even wanted that promotion. Sure it sounded good on paper, but her head hurt just thinking about the stress that would have come with it.

"It's been six months. It's time to bring this little pity party to a halt. We both know that you don't belong in Ouray."

"Not belong?" Tossing the pillow aside, she shot to her feet. "Are you kidding? This is the first place I've ever felt I *do* belong." She began to pace. "Back in Texas, I was merely existing. But here, I feel alive. I actually look forward to waking up every morning."

"Celeste—"

"You know what I did today?" She stopped and looked at her mother. "I took a meal to a friend who just had a baby. A simple act, but it was so gratifying. And then I held her baby while they ate. I've never held a baby before." She recalled every nuance, from Katelynn's little scrunched-up nose to that amazing baby smell. "Do you have any idea how relaxing that can be?"

"Not when they're screaming at the top of their lungs because of colic."

"Is that all you remember?" Had her mother ever looked on her with the same sense of awe Celeste had felt when holding baby Katelynn? Or had she always been a mistake, an interruption in her mother's well-planned life?

"Of course not, darling. You were a beautiful child. So full of promise. Always eager to please."

Because she was afraid her mother would end up hating her like she hated Celeste's father. As long as everything went according to her mother's plan, life was good.

Until Granny's death, Celeste had lived her whole life according to her mother's plan. A plan Hillary had laid out from the time Celeste was a little girl. What college she would go to, what she'd major in, what company she'd work for...

But moving to Ouray and reopening Granny's Kitchen was in no way part of that plan. Despite all of Celeste's success in the corporate world, this was the first time she'd taken control of her life. And she'd never been happier.

Looking at her mother, she suddenly wondered if following her dreams would end up costing her the love of the woman she'd worked her whole life to please.

If so, was it a sacrifice she was willing to make?

In the week and half since Gage and the girls had dinner at Celeste's, things had progressed smoothly. Despite Hillary's constant demands. Hillary said jump, Celeste asked how high. Yet whenever Celeste approached her about helping out, Hillary would come up with some lame excuse about not doing manual labor or that she was simply too busy with her own work.

Needless to say, Gage wasn't a fan of how she took advantage of Celeste's giving spirit.

Nonetheless, the restaurant had reopened and things were back on track with the upstairs units. The entire space had been gutted, plumbing had been reworked and new framing was being set into place. He'd even started looking forward to those times when Celeste would pop in unexpectedly to check on things. Though they weren't near as frequent as he'd like.

Seemed the more they were apart, the more he wished they were together. Just the admission of that drove him crazy.

Using a nail gun, he drove another nail into a stud. His attraction to the dark-eyed beauty with a heart as big as Texas was growing increasingly difficult to deny. Did he dare offer up his heart again? Not to mention those of his daughters?

"Gage?"

Oh, yeah. He was in trouble, all right. Just the sound of Celeste's voice brought a smile to his face.

The tapping of high heels against the wooden floor seemed louder than usual. Peering through a small forest of vertical two-by-fours, he observed that Celeste wasn't alone. Hillary was close behind, her expression one of vague curiosity as she scanned the space.

"Mom wanted to see how things were coming." Clad in dark gray slacks and a soft fuzzy red sweater, Celeste looked as pretty as ever. Though, he kind of preferred the jeans-and-boots look of last week.

"What do you think?" He gestured to the space with his free arm.

"This is so much brighter than I remember." Hillary twisted and turned, eyeing every corner. "I used to hate coming up here because it was so dark and depressing."

"Our goal is to utilize as much of the natural light as possible." He set the nail gun on the floor and moved toward the women. "Of course, once the walls go up, we'll lose a lot of it in the hallway."

"Gage suggested we increase the size of the window on the door and add some sidelights," said Celeste.

"Some LED lighting in the halls will help, too," he added.

"Oh, I hadn't thought about that. Good idea." The way Celeste smiled up at him made his pulse race.

She continued to walk her mother through the space, showing her how the rooms would be situated, along with the bathrooms and kitchenettes. Her excitement was hard to miss. And the glimmer it brought to her espresso eyes was incredibly appealing.

Forcing himself not to stare, he pretended to return to his work.

Celeste's cell phone rang.

"Hey, Karla." She paused. "Okay. I'll be right there." She tucked the phone back into the pocket of her slacks. "I need to get back downstairs."

"That's all right, darling. I'm sure Gage won't mind continuing the tour."

Celeste arched a questioning brow in his direction.

As if he could resist. "No. Of course not." Though Celeste had already covered most of the high points.

"Good." Celeste smiled and headed for the door. "Just come on back down when you're finished, Mom."

"All right, darling." Hillary waved then turned his way, wearing a smile that appeared a little too forced. "Shall we?"

Deciding to give her the benefit of the doubt, he moved into the area that would be the largest of the three suites and gestured to the far wall. "I believe Celeste has decided to leave the stone exposed here."

"That'll add a nice rustic charm." She ran a hand over the rough surface.

"We'll clean it up as much as we can, put some sealer on it."

"And what about flooring?"

"Celeste said she'd like to keep the original hardwood in the main part of the room. Of course, we'll sand and restain it, then we'll tile the kitchen and bath areas."

"Countertops?"

"Last I heard she wanted granite."

"Good. Good." Hillary's scrutiny continued.

"You know, Celeste designed this layout herself." For as much as he'd tried to object initially, he had to commend her. Her configuration made the most of each space and her drawing kept everything to scale.

"Doesn't surprise me. My daughter has always had an eye for the finer things in life."

He scuffed his boot across the time-worn floorboards. "I don't know about that, but she definitely knows what works and what doesn't."

"All of these upgrades will do wonders for the value of the building."

"I suppose. Though, I don't think Celeste is really concerned about that."

Hillary looked at him now. "Don't kid yourself. My daughter isn't serious about any of this."

"I'd have to politely disagree with you, Hillary. Celeste has put a great deal of time and effort into both the restaurant and these suites."

"Oh, I'm certain she has. What I meant was that this whole Ouray thing is nothing more than Celeste sowing some wild oats. Once this project is finished, she'll be bored in no time." She closed the short distance between them, her brown eyes alight with amusement. "You see, my daughter is used to the fast-paced life of the big city. And there's nothing in Ouray that could possibly compete with that."

A familiar ache wrapped around Gage's heart.

"Thank you for the tour, Gage." She started for the door. "Keep up the good work."

Gage watched the door close behind her. Could Hillary be right? The Celeste she described wasn't the woman he'd come to know. The Celeste he knew loved Granny's Kitchen, Ouray and its people. Then again, Hillary was her mother. She'd known Celeste far longer than he had.

He kicked at a scrap of wood and sent it flying across the room. He was such a fool. Hadn't Tracy taught him that a leopard didn't change its spots? Someone like Celeste would never be content in Ouray.

Drawing a large amount of air into his lungs, he closed his eyes and willed his anger to subside. He may have begun to open his heart, but at least he'd kept his mouth shut. Meaning that as far as Celeste was concerned, they were still nothing more than friends. He'd finish this job, keeping his private life as far away from Celeste as possible, and pray that by the time she said goodbye, his and his daughters' hearts were still intact.

Aside from the bear incident, Celeste wasn't one to panic. And since that event was life threatening, it didn't count. However, waking up to find a layer of snow covering the ground the day before the fall festival was enough to send her to the brink.

Kids shouldn't have to wear snow boots for a cake walk. They'd freeze in the bounce house. That is, if they even showed up at all.

She breathed deeply and closed her eyes. *Lord, You are the God of everything. You change times and seasons. Please, please, please let the fall festival be exactly that.*

Although, worst-case scenario, she supposed they could change it to a winter carnival.

Yeah, right. With pumpkins?

Grabbing the coffeepot, she moved from one table to the next, refilling cups as needed, all the while staring outside at the white flakes falling to the ground. Any other time, she would have relished the scene. Been excited even.

Out of the corner of her eye, she spotted Gage on his way up the stairs outside. Funny, he usually stopped to check in with her first and grab a cinnamon roll. His departure yesterday had been stealthy, too, and she couldn't help wondering why. She'd become so accustomed to him letting her know his comings and goings. Not that he needed to. Still, it was kind of nice.

After fifteen minutes with no sign of Gage, she left her waitress in charge and headed upstairs.

Butterflies took flight in her stomach, something she wasn't sure she'd ever felt before. Nor should she feel them now. Gage was her employee. So long as he was on the job, what concern was it of hers if he didn't stop and say good-morning?

None. Zip, zero, zilch.

But the part of her that had begun to think of Gage as more than a friend was really bugged. Which bugged her even more.

Reaching the small landing at the top of the stairs, she lifted her gaze to discover one of the most stunning views she'd ever seen. All around her, clouds obscured the snowy cliffs, while the jagged slopes and conifers looked as though they'd been dusted with powdered sugar.

A spectacular sight. One that she would enjoy so much more *after* tomorrow.

Turning, she reached for the door handle and paused. What was she going to say to Gage? Good morning? You forgot to check in?

She'd sound like a stalker.

The festival. That's right, he was supposed to drive to Montrose today and pick up the inflatables.

Inside, the sound of a lone hammer echoed through the space and the aroma of lumber filled her nostrils.

She spotted Gage, pounding nails into a board. Moving closer, she pointed to the nail gun on the floor. "I thought you said it was faster to use this?"

"Yep."

"Then why are you using a hammer?"

"What's the problem?" He looked at her now, his expression surly. "You in a hurry?"

"If you'll recall, I was hoping to have them ready in time for the ice—" Something wasn't right. "What's wrong with you?"

"Nothing." He set another nail to the wood and began pounding again.

She raised her voice. "Well, if this is nothing, I'd sure hate to see something."

The hammering halted and he glared at her.

"Come on, Gage. Talk to me." Taking a step closer, she laid a hand to his arm. "Something's bothering you."

His gaze fell to her hand, then lifted to her face. "When were you going to tell me?"

Clueless as to what he was talking about, she searched his midnight eyes for clues. "Tell you what?"

He pulled away now, tossed the hammer in his toolbox. "You know, your mother may have her faults, but at least she doesn't beat around the bush. She told me you were leaving."

"Leaving?" As much as she loved her mother, Celeste just might have to wring her neck. "Why would she tell you I'm leaving?"

"What is this, twenty questions?"

"Apparently, so just answer the question, Gage."

"No. Why don't *you* tell *me*? Or more importantly, why *didn't* you tell me?"

"Because there's nothing to tell. I'm not going anywhere." Except maybe to her condo to have it out with her mother. "All I want to do is get these suites finished so I can increase my revenue."

"And what about when they're done? What will you do then?"

"Same thing I've been doing. Except I'll need to add a housekeeper to the payroll."

"Aren't you afraid you'll get bored? That the excitement will wear off? Then you'll be stuck in boring little Ouray."

Her hands flew to her hips. "I happen to love boring little Ouray. *Especially* the boring part."

"Oh, yeah?" He took a step closer, his stubborn stance mirroring her own.

"Yeah." There was barely a hairbreadth between them. He was so close she could smell his soap, feel his breath on her skin.

Her heart raced as his eyes morphed into a deep sapphire and the muscle in his jaw relaxed.

She cleared her throat, dropping her hands to her side. "Would it…matter if I left?"

His hands dropped, too. "The town would lose their best cook."

"Oh." Disappointment had her gaze drifting away.

"Cassidy and Emma would miss you terribly." His tone was gentle this time.

Caught up in the moment, she threw caution to the wind.

"And what about you?" She forced herself to look him in the eye. "Would you miss me?"

Slowly, his fingers laced with hers, a smile tugging at the corners of his mouth. "More than I ever imagined possible."

Her heart soared, then plummeted just as quickly. What had she gotten herself into?

Chapter Eleven

No turning back now.

Gage had admitted how much he cared about Celeste. What was he thinking?

Simple. He was thinking about the way she made him smile. Her nurturing ways with his daughters. The fierce need to be with her whenever they were apart. And the inexplicable need to believe that a relationship with her could actually work.

In other words, he told the truth. It didn't hurt quite as bad as he expected. Where they went from here, though, he had no clue. At least they had the festival to keep them busy today.

What a day it was, too. The warm sun shone down on them while children of just about every age laughed and ran about. The smell of cotton candy, hot dogs and popcorn filled the air. In a word, perfection.

And Celeste was worried.

Okay, perhaps he was, too. A little anyway. Mostly that the day would be a muddy mess. But thanks to an overnight breeze, the park was mud-free.

Now, if he could figure out what to do about Hillary. He didn't know what transpired between her and Celeste last evening, only that Celeste was insistent this morning that her mother work the festival. Hillary, however, was not the least bit happy about Celeste's decision and had been complaining ever since she arrived.

He felt sorry for his mother, who'd offered to team up with Hillary at the cake walk. At last check, Hillary was taking tickets while his mom passed out treats to the winners. Maybe he should offer to take her place.

He started toward the large circle that was flanked by tables laden with baked goods.

"Hey there, Gage. Just the person I was hoping to see." His friend Ted came beside him with his eleven-year-old son. "Looks like a great turnout."

"Yeah, it is." Gage nodded, still shocked that they'd managed to pull it off in such a short amount of time. Thanks in large part to Celeste's organizational skills. Left to his own devices, the festival would have been a flop, but between the two of them, there wasn't a detail that hadn't been taken care of. He eyed the crystal-blue sky. "And we've got some great weather to boot."

Ted chuckled. "Good thing the festival wasn't yesterday."

"Dad, there's Austin and Zach." Ted's son pointed. "Can I hang out with them?"

"I reckon. You've got your tickets, right?"

"Yes, sir."

"All right, then, I'll be around here somewhere." Ted watched after the boy as he ran off. "I might have some news for you."

"From the mine?"

"Yep." Ted crossed his arms over his chest, his stance relaxed. "Rumor has it they're thinking about bringing on another foreman. You might want to give 'em a call or stop by. Let them know you're still interested."

Monday morning couldn't get here soon enough. Gage had been waiting for over a year for this kind of news. "Oh, you know I will, man. Thanks for letting me know."

"You and I have always been kindred spirits when it comes to the mines. It'd be a pleasure to finally work with you."

"Gage." He turned to see Blakely headed straight for him, along with her husband, Trent, who was pushing a stroller.

"Hey, Blakely."

"This is amazing." She spread her arms wide. "I can't believe you and Celeste did all of this. Now that's what I call teamwork."

"I'm afraid most of the credit goes to Celeste." His gaze searched out the woman in question, finding her at the ticket booth, smiling and looking like a model in those skinny jeans, low-heeled boots and a long gray sweater.

"Whatever the case, you two are putting me to shame. Austin has already informed me that this is the best fall festival ever."

Gage couldn't help but grin. "Good. I'm glad he's having fun."

A tiny whimper came from the stroller and both Trent and Blakely immediately stooped to investigate. Gage couldn't help looking, too. The sleeping pink bundle stretched and wriggled the way newborns do. Her face contorted as though she were about to let go a cry, then morphed into a smile.

"What's her name?" Ted addressed the proud parents.

"Katelynn Rose." Trent preened, settling his arm around his wife's shoulder. "Named after three of the most important women in our lives."

"Kate was Trent's mom," said Blakely. "Lynn was mine and, Rose is my grandmother, as well you know."

"Congratulations, you two." Ted shook Trent's hand, then gave Blakely a one-armed hug. "I need to run." He sent Gage an approving nod. "Hope to see you soon, buddy."

"Hi, Ted." The sound of Celeste's voice captured Gage's attention.

He turned to find her coming toward him.

"I was just complimenting Gage on what a wonderful job you guys did." Blakely stepped forward to meet Celeste's quick embrace.

"I know this is supposed to be for the kids, but y'all failed to tell me how much fun *I* was going to have." Celeste's espresso eyes twinkled with a childlike excitement he hadn't seen before. "I don't think I've *ever* had this much fun." Holding her hair back, she bent to peer into the stroller. Adjusted a blanket. "So precious." Straightening, she addressed Trent and Blakely. "How's she doing?"

"Couldn't be better," said Trent.

"Good." Celeste glanced over her shoulder, in the direction of the cake walk and her mother. "If you don't mind—" she regarded Trent and Blakely again "—I need to borrow Gage for a minute."

"Not at all," said a grinning Blakely. And the way her gaze darted between him and Celeste, Gage had a pretty good idea what she was thinking. What was it with women and matchmaking? "We need to track down Austin anyway."

Celeste started across the lawn, in the direction of the cake walk, and Gage followed. Her smile had diminished some and he couldn't help wondering why.

"I think I made a mistake," she said. "Insisting my mother help us. She's being downright rude."

He jammed his hands into his pockets. "Have you had any complaints?"

"No. But if I weren't in charge, I'd be complaining."

"You're probably just more sensitive to it since she's your mother."

"Oh, really?" She lifted a brow. "I heard her refer to this—" she swept a hand through the air, indicating the festival "—as 'pointless small-town nonsense.'"

Despite having heard a few of Hillary's remarks himself, he didn't want anything to ruin Celeste's fun. He stopped her at the far end of the prize table as the music began for another round of eager cake walk contestants. "Maybe you heard it out of context."

She looked at him through those long lashes. "Nice try."

The music stopped and people clapped for the lone victor.

His mom approached the table, winking at them as she retrieved a plate of chocolate cupcakes for the winner.

"See there? Maybe things aren't so bad after—"

A shriek cut through the air, followed by gasps and muffled giggles. Then everyone in the cake walk area fell silent.

Gage and Celeste pushed their way through the group to find Bonnie holding the now half-empty plate.

He rushed to her side. "Mom, what—?" His gaze moved to Hillary, who was standing just beyond his mother. His heart sank.

"I—I must have tripped." His mother looked from the plate to Hillary, her blue eyes wider than he'd ever seen them.

"She most certainly did not." Hillary spat out the words, attempting to wipe a blob of chocolate frosting from her cheek. Instead, she only made it worse. "That wretch did this on purpose."

"Mom…" Celeste struggled for composure, though she

was clearly amused. "There's no need for name-calling." She snagged a napkin someone held out and handed it to her mother before covering her grin.

Hillary, however, saw through her daughter's attempts, which only infuriated her all the more. "Did you see what she did to me?"

"Calm down, Mom. I'm sure it was an accident."

Hillary recoiled at the notion. "Accident, my eye!" She wiped her face and shirt until the napkin turned a dark brown, then let out a frustrated sigh. She glared at Gage's mother first, then those gathered around them. Finally, her attention returned to her daughter. "You are so much better than this, Celeste." Retrieving her clutch from under the table, she stuffed it under her arm and stormed out of the park.

Celeste pulled her Mustang into the garage, ready to give her mother a piece of her mind. The woman's behavior had been beyond embarrassing at the festival. Celeste still didn't know whether to laugh or cry over the great cupcake debacle. Honestly, the whole scene had been quite comical. If she'd seen it in a movie, she'd have laughed hysterically. Who didn't like it when the enemy got his or her comeuppance?

Unfortunately, this enemy was her mother and she couldn't help feeling at least a little bit sorry for her. No matter how much she deserved it.

Poor Bonnie. After the way Hillary acted, no one in their right mind would fault Bonnie for her momentary lapse in judgment. And yet she'd wholeheartedly extended a dinner invitation, determined to make things up to Hillary.

Now it was up to Celeste to talk her mother into accepting. Moving Mount Sneffels to Texas might be easier, but she'd promised Bonnie she would try.

She killed the engine, grabbed the pumpkin from her passenger seat and headed into the house, wondering why her mother was still here. Especially since she seemed to despise Ouray. Tomorrow would mark two weeks since her surprise arrival and as far as Celeste knew, she had no plans to leave anytime soon.

Talk about odd. Her mother had never been away from work this long. Although, technically, she was working via her laptop and cell phone, but still, Mom had never been away from one of Magnet Oil's offices for more than a day.

Upstairs, she found her mother sitting at the dining table, staring at her laptop, nursing a cup of coffee. Not a trace of frosting remained. Her hair was once again perfectly coifed, and a flowing white top made her black yoga pants look downright elegant.

Celeste set the pumpkin on one end of the table, uncertain where to start. Should she come out with guns ablaze or use a more tactful approach? One thing was certain, though, any sign of weakness or backing down and her mother would have the upper hand in no time.

"It appears the festival was a success." Her mother took another sip without looking up.

"For the most part."

"You always were good at organizing."

Celeste's nod acknowledged the matter-of-fact compliment.

"I suppose I owe you an apology." Mom closed her computer, moved her reading glasses to the top of her head and leaned back in her chair as she addressed Celeste. "I wasn't exactly approachable today."

"That's an understatement." Celeste pulled out a chair

to sit, then decided against it. When confronting someone, standing always intimated authority. "Sorry, Mom, but your behavior was deplorable. You had no right to come here and belittle Ouray like that."

Her mother straightened, lifted her chin. "You're right. I was out of line."

By the grace of God, Celeste managed to keep her jaw from dropping to the floor, but somebody needed to alert the newspapers, because Hillary Ward-Thompson never admitted she was wrong.

"It's not me you need to apologize to," said Celeste.

"Darling, surely you don't expect me to go door-to-door and apologize to *everyone*." Nothing like condescension to inspire a little heel digging.

"No. Just Bonnie." Celeste crossed her arms over her chest. "Despite your antics, she was nice enough to invite us to dinner."

Indignation narrowed her mother's gaze. "I am *not* setting foot in that woman's house."

"Yes, you will. And not only that, you will apologize to her for the way you behaved today."

"What if I refuse to go?"

"Then you may as well pack your bags and head home, because you're not going to stay with me." Though she meant every word, Celeste was shocked that she'd actually said them. She'd never stood up to her mother before.

"So you're going to choose a virtual stranger over me? The woman who gave you life."

"No. I'm choosing decency. And you should, too."

An hour later, Celeste pulled up in front of the Purcell home with her mother in the passenger seat. God was amazing. Yet she knew her mother well enough to keep praying that Hillary didn't have any sort of retaliation up her sleeve.

Gage emerged from the front door of the two-tone gray Victorian and started down the steps as they got out of the car.

Celeste couldn't help smiling. Not only because he looked amazing in that dusty-blue long-sleeved T-shirt, but because he was quickly becoming her rock. Someone she could count on to be there for her. A fact she found rather unsettling. Until now, the only person she'd been able to say that about was Granny.

"Welcome, ladies." He strolled toward them and offered his elbow to her mother. To Celeste's surprise, Hillary took it.

Perhaps she'd decided to play nice.

"What a beautiful house." Celeste admired the abundance of intricate millwork.

"Very lovely," her mother said. "Especially the stained glass."

Celeste's gaze drifted to the second-story windows that were bordered by pink, green and yellow glass.

"Believe it or not, they're original to the house," Gage added.

Bonnie and Phil, Gage's dad, met them in the foyer.

Celeste couldn't help noticing that Bonnie's hands were clasped so tightly that her knuckles were white.

"Celeste!" Emma bounced across the hardwood floors and thrust her little arms around Celeste's waist. "I'm so glad you're here."

"Me, too." Celeste stroked the child's hair. "Where's your sister?"

"Right here." Cassidy moved at a more leisurely pace, but still welcomed Celeste with a hug.

"I can't tell you how pleased I am that you could make it." Bonnie hugged Celeste, before moving in front of her mother. "Hillary, I owe you one doozy of an apology. I don't know what to say, except that I am so very sorry for humiliating you like that."

Hillary nodded, her shoulders rigid. "I was humiliated."

Celeste held her breath.

"But I deserved it. I was a bit unfiltered today and, for that, I apologize. I shouldn't have said those things."

The corners of Bonnie's mouth lifted, genuine this time as opposed to nervous. "Perhaps we should start over." She extended her hand. "It's a pleasure to meet you, Hillary. I'm Bonnie Purcell."

Over the next few minutes, the remaining members of the Purcell family arrived. Gage's sister, Taryn, her husband, Cash, and their dog, Scout. Shortly thereafter their older brother, Randy, his wife, Amanda, and their son, Steven, arrived. The men gravitated to the football game on TV in the living room, while the women gathered in the kitchen.

"Celeste, honey—" Bonnie wiped her hands then laid the towel on the granite-topped island "—could I get you to help me set the table?"

"Sure." Out of the corner of her eye, Celeste watched as Cassidy approached Hillary at the kitchen table.

"Mrs. Thompson?" asked Cassidy. "Would you play checkers with me?"

Celeste froze. Cassidy was a sensitive child. She didn't want to see her get her feelings hurt.

"Oh, I haven't played checkers in such a long time," her mother said.

Cassidy's shoulders dropped a notch. It must have taken all the courage the child could muster to voice her request.

Celeste took a step forward, then halted as her mother continued.

"So you'll have to go easy on me. Okay?"

Cassidy's smile nearly lit up the room and Celeste had to admit that her mother's wasn't far behind.

Thank You, God.

After helping Bonnie in the dining room, Celeste wandered across the foyer into the living room. Cheers and commentary sounded from the men parked on the leather sofas, while Emma and Steven tried to keep Scout from interfering with the Candy Land game they had spread across the floor.

At a small table in the corner, Hillary and Cassidy huddled around a wooden checkerboard. Mom moved a piece and then Cassidy promptly jumped it and added the game piece to her pile. Hillary pouted, but Celeste saw through it. Her mother was enjoying herself. For possibly the first time in who knows how long.

Celeste sighed. This was how a family, a home, should be. A safe haven filled with love and laughter.

This was what she'd wanted all her life. What she still longed for.

Her gaze inadvertently drifted to Gage, and her cheeks heated when she realized he'd been watching her.

He stood and came alongside her. "What's got you so dreamy-eyed?" The words were a tickle on her ear, sending a shiver of gooseflesh down her arms.

"Oh, noth—"

"Dinner's ready," Bonnie hollered from the dining room. Her timing couldn't have been better.

Celeste took a seat between Gage and her mother.

After prayer, Bonnie lifted her water glass. "A toast to Gage and Celeste for the best fall festival Ouray has ever seen."

"Here, here," echoed around the table.

Celeste dared a look at Gage, and the spark igniting in those deep blue eyes nearly knocked her out of her chair.

"Things may have started off a little rocky," he said, "but once we embraced our differences…" He took hold of her hand. "I think we make a pretty good team."

Celeste's heart pounded so wildly she could barely catch her breath. There was one thing she knew for certain.

She was falling in love with Gage Purcell.

Chapter Twelve

The following Wednesday morning, Gage found himself lamenting the fact that his helper, Logan, had called in sick. That meant the tape embedding fell solely on him, taking twice as long to complete. Throw in the fact that it was his least favorite part of any job and his good mood was rapidly diminishing.

The only bright spot was that he'd likely see Celeste a few times throughout the day. Seemed she'd had his emotions tangled in all kinds of knots since the festival. He'd not only come to expect her dropping in, he looked forward to it.

Just then, he heard the door open into the space above the restaurant, sending a jolt of anticipation coursing through his veins.

Since the drywall was now in place, he had to move into the hall to see who was coming. Not that he didn't have a pretty good idea already.

"Gage?"

He rounded the corner and almost collided with Celeste.

"I'm ready to help you tape and bed." She struck a pose and Gage couldn't help grinning like a love-struck teenager. She wore torn jeans, sneakers and a ratty sweat-shirt, and her ponytailed hair was covered with a faded Cowboys baseball cap. In a word, gorgeous.

"Have you ever done tape embedding before?"

"No. Is it hard?"

"Not really, though it does take some practice. And it's messy."

"That much I figured." She glanced at her clothing. "Which is why I'm dressed this way."

"Then I'd say you're perfect for the job." Returning to the corner suite, he knelt beside the five-gallon bucket of joint compound and pried the lid off, all the while trying to settle his racing pulse. Funny, he'd allowed other customers to work with him before and none had ever had this effect on him. Then again, they weren't Celeste. And the fact that she'd changed her plans, along with her clothes, to help him did strange things to his heart.

"This—" he removed the lid "—is why it's so messy."

She eyed the thick white mixture. "Looks like frosting."

"Yeah, but I can guarantee it doesn't taste like frosting."

"That's probably a good thing."

He sent her a curious look.

"You'd always run out, because Emma would eat it all."

He laughed. "This is true." Standing, he gestured to the walls. "Okay, so we've got our drywall up. But you see all the nails and seams?"

"Yes."

"We're going to cover those up so we're left with one smooth surface." He loaded his trowel with a blob of mud.

Celeste watched closely as he spread the joint compound over the horizontal section where two pieces of drywall came together. Her proximity sent a waft of vanilla fragrance swirling around him, making it difficult to concentrate, but he still managed a straight line.

"Now we're going to take this tape—" he reached for the roll of paper tape that dangled from his belt and pulled out a length "—and carefully lay it over the seam, pressing just enough to keep it in place."

"So use a light touch?"

"Very. Because I'll use my taping knife to embed the tape into the mud by gently dragging it across the tape." He demonstrated, then stepped back to admire his handiwork.

"I get it now. You *embed* the tape. So it's tape embedding, not tape and bedding."

"You are one smart cookie, Miss Thompson." He offered her his taping knife. "Ready to give it a try?"

She took a deep breath. "Ready as I'll ever be." She took hold of the knife. "What if I do it wrong?"

"Don't worry. The mud doesn't dry instantly, so you've got time to fix any mistakes." He watched as she slid the six-inch knife across the next seam, impressed yet again by her willingness to step in and help. Tracy had been all about Tracy. She never volunteered to help him with anything unless it benefited her.

An hour later, he and Celeste were each working their own wall, though he stayed in the same room just in case she had any problems.

"So who's minding things downstairs?" He glanced over his shoulder.

Celeste was on a ladder, tackling a vertical seam near the ceiling. "Karla and Leslie."

"Leslie? That's your new waitress, right?"

"Yes. And she's definitely a keeper."

Funny. Gage was beginning to think the same thing about Celeste.

He shook his head. *Lord, are You sure about this? Because falling in love again has never been on my radar.*

Sneaking another peek at the woman in question, he saw her start down the ladder. She missed the last rung, though, landed hard and stumbled backward, running into him.

Turning, he caught her by the arm. "You okay?"

"Just call me Grace." She chuckled.

He couldn't help smiling. "So does joint compound also work as a facial masque?"

"What?"

He tapped his nose to indicate she had some on hers, and her eyes crossed as she tried to look, which made him laugh all the more.

"Here, let me help you." He tugged the rag from his back pocket and wiped away the wayward blob. "There. You're back to beautiful." He shrugged, realizing what he'd insinuated. "Not that you ever left."

A shy smile graced her lips and her cheeks turned pink. "Thank you."

"No. Thank you. You didn't have to help me, you know?" He inched closer, taking hold of her free hand. His heart felt like a jackhammer against his chest. "But I'm glad you did."

She peered up at him with those dark eyes that made him feel as though whatever was going on between them was really possible. That *they* were possible.

Sounds of an old-fashioned telephone echoed through the empty room, ruining the moment. Celeste took a step back as he yanked his cell from his hip.

"Hello."

"Gage. This is Tom Milner from Branson Mining."

Turning toward the window, Gage quickly forced his mind to shift gears. "Yes, sir."

"We're looking for a foreman for the Golden Girl mine and were wondering if you might be available to come by our office Friday afternoon for an interview. Say one o'clock?"

Gazing down on Main Street, he mentally sifted through his calendar. "That should be fine."

"Excellent. We'll see you then."

Gage ended the call, stupefied. After all this time. And a foreman position, at that.

"This is amazing." He faced Celeste again.

"What is?"

"That was Branson Mining. They want to interview me for a job."

Her mouth fell open. "Gage, that's wonderful. That's what you've been waiting for."

"I know." He ran a hand through his hair, still in disbelief. Then he looked around the room, reality smacking him in the face. "Uh-oh."

"What?"

"This." He swept the barely roughed-in room with his arm. "If I get the job with the mine, there's no way I'll be able to finish this by January. Between the girls and work—"

She stopped him with a hand to his chest. "Gage, ever since you told me you were a miner and that you were merely biding your time as a contractor, I knew this was a possibility."

"But we have a contract."

"Oh, who cares about some silly old contract? I have something better." She smiled up at him.

"What's that?"

"A plan."

His gaze narrowed. "What kind of plan?"

"Do you think you could have *one* of the suites complete before the ice festival? And maybe the entryway and hall?"

He contemplated the timeline. "Probably." He'd have to get his mother to help with the girls, though.

"And don't worry about Cassidy and Emma. They can hang out with me."

"How did you know I was thinking about them?"

She sent him an incredulous look. "Since when have you not put their needs first?"

That made him grin again. "Point taken."

"Good. Okay, so I've already committed one of the units for the ice festival, but I can pull the ads for the rest. Which means I won't need them ready until the high season. Do you think you could have everything completed by May?"

He was not only impressed but beyond appreciative that she'd thought this out. "That I know I can do."

"Great. Then I guess that leaves just one more thing."

"What's that?"

She took a step closer. "Do you think you'll be meeting your friends up at Bachelor-Syracuse anytime soon?"

"We have nothing planned. Why?"

Pink tinged her cheeks once again. "I'd like you to take me into the mine."

"But I thought you were claustrophobic."

"Mind over matter, right?" She shrugged it off. "I want to see what you do. Why you're so passionate about mining. Besides, as long as you're with me, I know I'll be okay."

There went that jackhammer again. Celeste might be okay, but his heart was in big trouble.

"You're sure you want to do this?"

Celeste tightened her grip on Gage's hand Thursday morning, determined not to let this mine tunnel get the best of her. People had been going in and—more importantly—out of here for over a hundred years. They did tours, for crying out loud. Which meant she had nothing to fear.

So why were her palms so sweaty?

Not very attractive. Still, that didn't stop Gage from holding on to her. For that, she was grateful.

"I'm sure." And she really was. She wanted to do this for Gage. To see what it was that put a spark in his eye whenever he talked about mining.

Unfortunately, that meant walking some fifteen hundred feet into a mountain.

"You're not very convincing." He stopped them and turned to look at her, killing the headlamp on his helmet. "I appreciate that you're willing to do this, but you don't—"

"Yes. I do." She shrugged. "It's a silly fear that I need to overcome. Besides, I really want to see this world through your eyes."

Wearing a childlike grin, he gave her hand a squeeze. "Then I guess I'd better make things interesting enough to take your mind off of your fears."

"I'm counting on it."

He clicked his headlamp on again as they continued.

She drew in a deep breath, forcing herself to study her surroundings. The sandstone tunnel actually wasn't as narrow as she'd imagined it would be. Twelve to fifteen feet across, perhaps. Maybe ten to twelve feet high.

The air was damp, though not musty or unpleasant, as drops of water trickled down the walls.

"What's that yellowish-white coating on the walls?" Thicker in some areas, it had kind of an icy appearance.

"That's calcite." He paused and, since they were a good fifteen feet away from the nearest lightbulb, aimed his gazillion-watt flashlight at the wall for a better look. "A by-product of water continuously trailing over the same area. You're welcome to touch it."

She stepped across the old rails that Gage had said once carried the ore cars in and out of the mine and ran a hand over the surface. To her surprise, it wasn't slick at all, but porous. "I guess it's the calcium in the water that causes it?"

"Exactly." He again offered his hand as she returned to his side. "Are you warm enough?"

His concern made her heart stutter. *As long as you keep holding my hand.*

She tugged at the hem of her jacket. "No complaints here." Nerves aside, with the mine at a constant temperature of fifty-five degrees, it was warmer in here than it had been outside.

"Mines have a lot of different levels," said Gage. "We're on level nine, which means there are eight levels beneath us."

"Wow. How do they get from one level to the next?"

"Elevators, which used to be steam powered, ladders and tunnels. Believe it or not, there's an entire infrastructure inside the mountain. That's where my job comes in."

"How do you know where to go? I mean, to dig the tunnels."

"Easy. We follow the vein."

"Vein?"

He aimed his flashlight at the wall. "See this line?" He highlighted a half-inch-wide thread that angled upward. "Yes."

"That's a vein. If they found one that was gold, silver or some other desired mineral, then they'd start dynamiting to create a drift or tunnel."

"You mean they dynamited this tunnel?"

"Over a hundred years ago, at the lightning-fast speed of three feet per day."

She glanced at the expanse in front of, then behind her. "It must have taken them forever to make this."

"Pretty much."

"Do you still use dynamite today?"

"Yes." He started walking again, seemingly unfazed by the fact. "Though we no longer use the rod-and-hammer method. Larger mines will use special boring machines. Either way, excavating tunnels nowadays is much faster."

Some fifty feet later, Celeste saw something that sent a chill down her spine. While the tunnel continued, a gate bearing a DANGER: KEEP OUT sign now spanned its width.

"What's back there?" She slowed her pace, still clinging tightly to Gage's hand.

"A cave-in."

That stopped her dead in her tracks. *"A what?"*

"Don't worry." He tugged her against him, his smile coaxing. "We're going in here."

She followed him into what appeared to be a room on one side of the tunnel. In it was a bench and some old mining equipment, and one of the walls was covered with one-inch holes.

Gage proceeded to explain how miners lived a hundred years ago. How they worked by the light of a solitary candle, one man wielding a sledgehammer, while another held a steel rod. Working together, they'd drive the rod deep enough to insert a stick of dynamite.

After lighting a candle that was perched near the wall, he reached for her hand. "Do you trust me, Celeste?"

Peering into Gage's sapphire eyes, she realized just how much she'd come to trust him. Probably more than she'd ever trusted anyone before. He was a man of honor. "Of course."

Suddenly, they were in utter darkness, save for the candle flickering against the wall.

She sucked in a breath.

"It's okay. I've got you." He slid his arm around her waist and held her close. "Close your eyes for five seconds. Give them a chance to adjust."

She complied, her breathing evening out.

"Okay. Open them."

While still dim, the whole room appeared illuminated now, yet only from that single candle.

"This is how they worked?"

"Yep. So the man holding the hammer would aim for the shine." He pointed to the end of the rod. "And that's how they got the job done."

"Incredible." She puffed out a laugh. "Makes me feel like such a wimp."

Placing a finger under her chin, he tilted her face to look at him. "You are hardly a wimp, Celeste. You left your life in Texas to start a new one in Ouray. That took a lot of courage."

"I could say the same about you." She laid a hand against his chest. Felt his heartbeat beneath her fingers. "Coming back here with the girls."

"Yeah, but I grew up here, so it's not the same."

"If you say so."

He grinned. "Thank you for allowing me to share this with you. It's not exactly what I do, but it gives you a little insight." His arm tightened around her. "You're not shaking anymore."

"I have you to thank for that."

He lowered his head, then hesitated. "I really want to kiss you."

She couldn't help smiling as a lightness filled her chest. "Good. Because I really wish you would."

Eliminating the short distance that remained, he touched his lips to hers. So sweet. So tender. So incredibly right.

With both of his arms wrapped around her waist, Celeste had never felt safer. The protectiveness that enveloped her was something she'd never known before. Something she wanted to last forever. Like Cinderella and her Prince Charming.

But nothing lasted forever. Or so she'd been told.

Question was, what did she believe?

Gage ended the kiss, brushed his nose against hers and smiled. "Clay is probably wondering about us." He turned the lights back on and she immediately missed the warmth of his embrace.

"I need to get back anyway. Mom's planning to have lunch at the diner."

"How are things going with your mother?" he asked a while later as they drove back into town.

"Good, actually. She's stopped hounding me about moving back to Texas, so I think, maybe, she's finally come to accept my decision." She prayed that was the case anyway.

Her mother was waiting when they arrived at Granny's Kitchen. Gage headed upstairs to check on Logan while Celeste joined her mother at a booth for some baked potato soup.

"How was your morning?" She eyed her mother across the table.

"Wonderful, darling." Hillary dipped her spoon into her bowl. "I met with a real estate agent who told me that Granny's Kitchen is prime real estate. She said that if you were to sell, she'd have no problem getting top dollar."

Chapter Thirteen

"All right, Mom. What gives?"

Celeste had been waiting all day to have this conversation with her mother. Since she'd been gone most of the morning at the mine with Gage, she didn't want to burden her waitstaff by asking them to carry the afternoon shift as well, and this definitely wasn't the kind of conversation they could have at the restaurant. Now, though, she stormed into her living room and glared down at her mother.

"Anger doesn't become you, Celeste." With a cup of coffee in one hand, Mom sat back in the overstuffed chair, adjusting her long silk robe to cover her crossed legs. "You wouldn't want those worry lines to become permanent, now, would you?"

Not once in her twenty-nine years had Celeste wanted to scream so badly. But nearly three weeks of her mother's button pushing was about to send her over the edge.

"Why did you go behind my back and talk to a real estate agent?"

"I'm only looking out for your best interest, darling." She fingered the corner of a paperback book that was sitting on the arm of the chair. "One of these days you're going to come to your senses. I just want you to be prepared, that's all."

Celeste's gaze narrowed. "I came to my senses the day I decided to move to Ouray."

Avoiding eye contact, her mother sipped her coffee. "I hear more snow is in the forecast."

"Stop trying to change the subject." Celeste unbuttoned her peacoat. "I don't care if we're up all night, we're going to get to the bottom of this once and for all."

"The bottom of what, dear?"

"Don't play innocent with me. I know you, remember?" Celeste took off her coat and tossed it on the sofa. "Why are you still here?"

Her mother looked stunned. Perhaps even hurt. "You don't want me here?"

Celeste refused to back down. "No, I did not say that. But you know good and well that this is not your MO. You don't take vacations, you can't stand to be away from the office and you despise Ouray."

"So, I needed a break." Hillary ran a finger around the rim of her cup. "And I do not despise Ouray."

"You could have fooled me. Not to mention everyone else who was at the festival." Celeste took a deep breath and sat on the arm of the couch. "Okay, fine. I'll give you the benefit of the doubt. That still doesn't give you the right to come out here and start trying to run my life. A life I chose and happen to enjoy a great deal."

"For now."

"No, Mom. Like it or not, this is the real me." She crossed her arms. "I'm finally living the kind of life *I* want. I'm sorry if that disappoints you, but Ouray is my home now."

Her mother moved to the edge of her seat, looked directly at Celeste. "You are so gifted. *So* intelligent. I had so many plans for you."

With a calm that had always been her greatest asset, she said, "Many are the plans in a man's heart, but it's the Lord's purpose that prevails."

Her mother rolled her eyes. "Now you sound like your grandmother."

"I don't think that's such a bad thing."

Her mother stood, moved to the French doors in the dining room and stared into the darkness.

She could try to run away all she wanted, but Celeste was determined to end this tonight. She'd lived her whole life according to her mother's plan, and yet the woman always expected more. A cycle that had taken a toll on Celeste, both physically and mentally.

These past several months, though, had taught her that she had to live the life God had called her to. Not her mother. And she would not back down.

She shoved to her feet and followed. "Mom, you can't—"

"I just don't know how I fit into your life anymore." Her mother's voice was so soft she almost didn't hear her.

Shocked by the declaration, Celeste braced herself against the pass-through. "What do you mean?"

Her mother turned then, her eyes moist with unshed tears. Something Celeste had never seen before. "This is all—" Mom waved a hand through the air. "—so different. And what I tried so hard to break free of."

"Mom, it's not like you had a horrible childhood."

"I know." She set her cup on the table. "But Ouray was too small for me. I was so…driven, so determined to make a name for myself. Your grandmother may have been content to play Suzy Homemaker, but I didn't want to rely on someone else to take care of me. Then I met your father." She paused, as though collecting her thoughts. "Oh, how he used to make me laugh. He was one of those people that other people wanted to be around because he made you feel so good."

Celeste remembered that, too. Whenever she was down, she could count on her father to cheer her up.

"Still, I had no intention of marrying him. Then I got pregnant with you." She met Celeste's gaze now. "Your father was raised to do the honorable thing. He promised that I could still have my career and he'd take care of you. Apparently, he forgot that when he decided to take up with his secretary." Mom snagged her cup again and headed into the kitchen for a refill.

But not before Celeste saw the hurt in her mother's eyes.

She rounded the peninsula. "You loved him, didn't you?"

Cradling her mug, Mom nodded. "I didn't realize how much until he was gone."

Celeste didn't know what to say. She'd never heard any of this before. Never imagined the woman who told her not to waste her tears on a man was actually hurting. And why she refused to let go of her now.

"Mom…?" She moved beside her mother. "Are you afraid of losing me, too?"

Her mother nodded as silent tears spilled onto her cheeks.

"Oh, Mom." She wrapped her arms around the woman, careful not to bump her coffee. "You could never lose me. Don't you realize that without you and everything you taught me, I wouldn't have had the courage to take this leap and move to Ouray?" Releasing her hold, she pulled back. "You made me the woman I am today."

"You mean that?"

"With all my heart."

Setting her cup on the counter, her mother embraced

her, holding Celeste's head against her shoulder like she did when she was a child. "I do love you, darling. More than you will ever know."

"I know you do, Mom. However—"

Her mother let go then and Celeste faced her.

"—you have got to stop scheming and trying to force me to come back to Texas." She took hold of her mother's hands. "I want to enjoy our time together, not be at odds with one another."

Mom sniffed. "You really have done a wonderful job with the restaurant."

"You think so?"

"Yes. And the suites are a stellar idea." Her mother placed a hand on each side of Celeste's face and smiled. "You're a pretty savvy businesswoman."

Celeste's heart swelled. "Does this mean you'll stay a while longer?"

"Yes. And who knows, I might even help out at the restaurant."

He got the job.

Gage still couldn't believe they hired him on the spot, saying his credentials were beyond their expectations and his former boss had highly recommended him. Best of all, he could start on Monday.

He could hardly wait to share the news with Celeste. As he drove back into town, his heart pounded with anticipation. This called for a celebration, and he wanted to celebrate with Celeste. Maybe they could have their first real date. Considering he'd already kissed her, he'd kind of put the cart before the horse. Then again, dating wasn't the same when children were involved.

He found himself laughing out loud. For more than a year, he'd said he would never marry again. Now here he was talking about dating. And what was the point in dating if marriage wasn't a possibility? Yet the thought of a future with Celeste somehow seemed so right.

"Lord, Your ways are higher than my ways." His grip tightened on the steering wheel. *Thank You for bringing Celeste into my life.*

Retrieving his cell, he called his mother. "Hey, Mom, how would you feel about spending some time with your granddaughters tonight?"

Lucky for him, everything fell into place. Cassidy and Emma were spending the night with his parents, Celeste got someone to cover the restaurant for her and now he was escorting her into the Beaumont Grill for dinner. Man, if he thought she looked good before…wow! The figure-skimming dress she wore tonight nearly knocked his socks off. And he always liked it when she wore her long hair down, spilling over her shoulders.

The hostess seated them at a table near the fireplace and handed them their menus.

"Thank you." Celeste looked at him as the hostess disappeared. "I haven't been here before." Amidst the dim lighting, he watched as her gaze skimmed the tin ceiling and exposed brick wall. "This is really nice."

"One of Ouray's finer dining establishments." He quickly caught himself. "Not that Granny's Kitchen isn't great."

"It's okay. I know what you meant. They probably don't serve meat loaf." She smiled and studied her menu. "You look very dapper tonight."

He'd worn a light blue button-down shirt over a pair of dark wash jeans. Not a big deal, but to have Celeste notice did strange things to him. "Only because you're with me."

After placing their order, she laid her napkin in her

lap and leaned forward, resting her arms on the wooden table. "So, are you excited about the job?"

"Beyond excited is more like it. I've waited so long for this."

"I know you have. But God's timing is perfect and now He's placed you in the job you wanted."

"That's right. And if it had happened sooner, I wouldn't have met you."

Her cheeks reddened. "We live right across the street from each other, so we were bound to meet eventually."

"Perhaps." Reaching across the table, he took hold of her hand. "But we wouldn't have been forced to spend so much time together."

"Oh, so you're being forced to spend time with me?"

"You know what I mean." He stroked the back of her hand with his thumb. "You've brought something into the girls' and my lives that we haven't had for a long time. If ever. It's going to be tough not seeing you every day."

"You'll still see me. At least I certainly hope so."

"Yeah, I've still got the suites to finish. But even if didn't…" He squeezed her hand, inching closer. "You mean a lot to me, Celeste."

"Who had the beef tips?"

Gage looked up to see their server holding two plates. "That was quick." He let go of Celeste and leaned back in his chair to make room for the plate.

"And the osso buco." The server set the dish in front of Celeste. "Can I get you anything else?"

Gage glanced at Celeste first, noted the shake of her head, then looked at the waitress. "I think we're good."

He again reached his hand across the table. "Do you mind if I say a blessing?"

A soft smile caressed her lips. "Not at all."

He bowed his head. "Lord, thank You for this day.

Thank You for Your provision and that You are a God of immeasurable abundance. We ask that You would bless this food to the nourishment of our bodies. Amen."

"Amen." Celeste picked up her fork and took a small bite. "Mmm…" She swallowed, then pointed her utensil at the plate. "This is delicious."

"You sound surprised."

"I guess I am. I mean, who would expect to find such amazing osso buco in Ouray?" She grabbed another forkful. "I'm going to have to tell Mom about this."

He picked up his water. "Speaking of your mother. How did things go last night?"

"Quite interesting, actually." She wiped her mouth with the linen napkin. "I gained some real insight into my mother."

"Really." He cut another piece of beef. "Such as?"

"Well, I've always thought she was rather unaffected when my father left. She'd always tell me that we were better off without him and that we didn't need a man to take care of us." She paused, picked up her fork again. "Turns out my father's infidelity and subsequent departure left my mother with a gaping wound. I felt sorry for her."

"It's tough to be abandoned by someone that you love." Still, he'd seen Hillary take advantage of Celeste's tender heart before.

"Yes, it is." Compassion and understanding filled her brown eyes.

He set his fork down. "I'm not trying to sound unfeeling, but how does all of that play into her trying to get you back to Texas?" Or was Hillary simply trying to use her daughter's sympathy to save herself?

"It took me a while, but I finally figured it out. Ever since my dad left, Mom has planned out my whole life for me. School, college, my major. That was her way of expressing love. So when I rejected that plan and chose something else, she thought I was rejecting her."

"I guess that does shine some light on things." He studied the woman across from him. "I can only assume you set her straight."

"I did." She grinned. "She even told me I was a savvy businesswoman."

He could tell her mother's words had meant a lot. "I believe she's right."

After dinner, they donned their coats and moved into the cool night air.

"Where would you like to go now?" he asked.

"Would you be up for a stroll down Main Street?" The way she looked up at him through those long lashes, he'd have gone anywhere. "I rarely get the chance."

"By all means, let's go." He offered his elbow, then tugged her close when she took hold, covering her gloved hand with his.

They wandered past the window displays, pausing at one that had already been decorated for Christmas. Kind of early, if you asked him. Thanksgiving was still three weeks away.

"So what do the girls want for Christmas?" Celeste's gaze roamed the bountiful display of holiday decor.

"Pretty much everything they see in television commercials."

Her attention shifted to him, a question lifting one brow.

"Okay, maybe that's only true of Emma." He chuckled. "Honestly, I have no idea."

"Well, you'd better start figuring it out, Mister. What if one of them wants this year's hottest-selling toy? If you wait until December, it might be sold out."

"That would make for some sad faces on Christmas morning, wouldn't it?"

"Yes, it would. Is that a chance you're willing to risk?"

That made him laugh. "You know, for someone who isn't a parent yet, you're pretty smart."

Her smile faltered. She looked away.

He slid an arm around her waist. "That's only one of the things I love about you. You're always thinking of others."

Her gaze jerked to his, a puzzled look on her face. Then he realized what he'd said.

Never would he have imagined that he could feel this way about someone he'd known for little more than a month. Though he also knew that when God was part of the mix, things didn't always make sense.

He caressed Celeste's cheek and lost himself in her espresso eyes. "It's true. Somewhere along the way, I've fallen in love with you, Celeste." Before she could respond, he lowered his head and kissed her, praying she felt the same way.

Chapter Fourteen

Gage's words had played continuously on a loop through Celeste's mind for almost a week now. Yet for as much as she longed to reciprocate his declaration of love, she simply couldn't. Love was about trust and honesty. Respect. How could he trust her when she hadn't respected him enough to be completely honest?

Of course, he had no idea she was hiding something. Only God knew. And in His infinite mercy and grace, He'd forgiven her mistakes. Still, she had to tell Gage before they could even think of any kind of future together.

So, she made arrangements to drop by his house Thursday night after work. The girls would be in bed, so she and Gage could have an uninterrupted conversation.

However, as she stood on Gage's front porch, it became clear that the girls were not in bed after all. Giggles and the sound of little running feet seeped through the door.

Thoughts of Cassidy and Emma made her smile. Perhaps spending a few minutes with them would calm her nerves and make it easier for her to talk to Gage once they were tucked into bed.

She knocked on the door and a moment later, she was greeted by two pajama-clad, red-faced little girls.

"Celeste! Help me!" Gage stumbled to the door, every bit as winded as the girls. "They've been chasing me all night. You gotta make them stop."

"Nuh-uh." The girls chimed simultaneously.

"He's a tickle monster," said Emma through her giggles.

"And he's trying to catch us." Cassidy squealed and took off across the room with her sister and father close behind.

Celeste hurried inside and closed the door. "I'll save you, girls." She ditched her coat and joined in the pursuit. She followed them into the girls' bedroom, where Gage fell to the floor and his daughters piled on top of him. "Girls, there's only one way to slay the tickle monster."

They both looked at her.

"We have to tickle him." She lunged into the melee, sending Gage into fits of laughter as they relentlessly attacked him.

A few minutes later, they all collapsed, the sounds of heavy breathing filling the room.

"That was fun," said Emma as Celeste coaxed her to her feet.

"No." Gage pushed onto his knees. "That was exhausting."

"Have you two brushed your teeth?" Celeste looked at Emma first, then Cassidy.

"Yes, ma'am," they echoed.

"Good. Now hop into your beds." As she pulled the covers over Cassidy and Gage did the same for Emma, it struck her that if things worked out between her and Gage, she'd be a part of this every night. She didn't know if she was equipped to be a mother, but what a blessing it would be to claim these two little girls as her daughters.

"Will you read to us?" Emma's request was followed by a yawn.

"Not tonight, sweetie." Celeste gave her a hug and kiss good-night. "But maybe next time, okay?"

"Okay." With that, Emma rolled over and closed her eyes.

Celeste duplicated the bedtime ritual with Cassidy, as did their father, and headed for the door. "Good night, girls."

Gage flipped the light off and followed her into the hall, taking hold of her hand. "So what's your trick?"

"Trick?"

"Not one argument from Emma about reading." He rubbed the back of his neck with his free hand. "She usually hounds me until I give in."

Celeste smiled, turning to face him as the entered the living area. "That's because she knows you'll give in."

"You're probably right." He let go of her hand and started toward the kitchen. "Can I get you some water?"

"No, thank you."

"I'll be right back."

In his absence, she made herself at home on the sofa, kicking off her shoes and drawing her legs up under her. *Lord, give me the courage to say what I have to say.*

"How are things going up at the mine?" She asked when he returned. Since he'd started his new job, they really hadn't had much opportunity to talk.

"Incredible." He set his cup on the coffee table and joined her on the couch. "It's as though I never missed a beat from my job back in Denver."

"That's wonderful."

She'd never seen Gage as animated as he was when he told her all he'd been doing, about his coworkers and the mine itself. The way his face brightened as he spoke told her how happy he was to be doing what he loved. And she couldn't be happier for him.

Eventually, the conversation shifted back to her and how much they'd missed seeing each other.

"You were great with the girls. The way you just joined in, it's like you belong." He touched her cheek. "Can I ask you something?"

"Sure."

"Though I think I already know the answer." He straightened. "How do you feel about kids? I mean, like, being a mother."

Her heart screeched to a grinding halt. The time had finally come.

"I love kids. And if God called me to be a mother, I would consider it an honor." She reached for Gage's hand. "However, before we start talking about things like that, there's something I have to tell you."

"Okay." He looked perplexed. "Should I be worried?"

"No. At least, I don't think so." She shifted slightly. "Remember I told you how my whole life had been planned out?"

"Yeah."

"Well, sometimes even well-laid plans can get a kink in them." She tilted her head to look at him. "That kind of happened to me my junior year of college."

Her stomach churned. Her mouth went dry, making her wish she'd accepted that water.

"I guess my mother isn't the only one who was messed up by my father's betrayal."

"What do you mean?"

"My mother is a planner to the utmost degree. Always has been. Somehow I got it in my little eight-year-old brain that my mother hated my father because he did something that wasn't part of the plan. Keep in mind that, at that time, I didn't know he was having an affair. I just knew that he left."

Gage nodded.

"So I got it in my head that as long as I did things according to plan, my mother would still love me. But if I didn't…"

"Based on some of the things you've told me, I can see where you might think that."

"Everything was progressing the way it was supposed to. I was top of my class at the University of Texas, Mom was already scouting jobs for me…when I got pregnant."

"I see." Gage cocked his head, his gaze narrowing, though not in a bad way. "Did you tell your mother?"

"Are you kidding me? She would have been done with me for sure. Or so I thought anyway." Uneasy, she pushed to her feet and started to pace. "I panicked. And even though I knew it was wrong…" She stopped and made sure she had Gage's full attention. "I had an abortion."

Gage didn't say a word. He just sat there, his expression vacant.

She sat down beside him once again. "I can't tell you how ashamed I am. But I hope you understand why I had to tell you."

Straightening, he gripped the edge of the cushions, the rise and fall of his chest suddenly more pronounced. "So you got rid of a child because it stood in the way of your plans?" He didn't look at her.

"Yes." She stared at her clasped hands, embarrassed and waiting for him to say that he understood. That everyone made mistakes. That it didn't change the way he felt about her.

Instead, he pushed to his feet. Picked up her coat. "You should go."

His words cut her as deep as any knife.

Disbelief, along with an unbearable ache, settled into her chest as she shoved her feet into her shoes. She stood and accepted her coat, all the while battling tears.

"I think it would best if we didn't see each other anymore." He looked at her now, pain evident in his darkened eyes. "My daughters were sacrificed once at the altar of somebody's dreams. I can't risk that happening again."

"Gage, I would never…"

Try as she might, she couldn't stop her bottom lip from trembling. How could he even think she'd do anything to hurt Cassidy and Emma?

A sob escaped her throat, but she covered it with her hand. The thought of not seeing Gage was bad enough, but not seeing Cassidy and Emma was too much to bear.

She reached for the door, not even bothering to put on her coat. Continuing outside, she heard Gage move behind her. Would he try to stop her? Perhaps he simply needed time to process things.

"And you should probably find another contractor to finish the suites, too."

By Friday morning, Gage felt as though his heart had been run over by a lawn mower.

Leaning back in his desk chair, he rubbed the ache in his forehead. The look of disbelief and anguish on Celeste's face when he sent her away had taunted him all night. He loved her, of that he was certain. But she'd selfishly chosen her aspirations over her child, just like Tracy. And that he could not ignore.

To contemplate a future with Celeste would be like playing with fire. Eventually, he'd get burned. Not only him, but Cassidy and Emma, as well.

Good thing he'd found out now. Suppose he'd married Celeste and then she decided that motherhood wasn't for her?

At least this way he wouldn't have to worry about the possibility of his children being abandoned again. Even though they'd bounced back from their mother's betrayal, he couldn't help wondering what kind of scars it had left on their hearts. How it would affect them as they grew older. Especially Cassidy, who had a tendency to internalize things. If he'd married Celeste and she turned her back on them, the repercussions would be disastrous.

Celeste isn't Tracy.

Maybe. But he couldn't chance it. Even if his own heart was in shambles.

"You ready to check on that new drift?"

Looking up, he saw Ted standing in the doorway of the mine office.

"Sure." Gage chugged the rest of his coffee, grateful for the distraction.

The old wooden swivel chair creaked as he stood. He gathered his hard hat, safety glasses and mine light.

They'd recently blasted out a new tunnel in the mine and, now that it had been mucked or had the rocky debris removed, the integrity of the space needed to be inspected for any loose spots that could give way later and, potentially, harm equipment or workers. That meant he had to have his wits about him, not allowing his mind to dwell on something that would never be.

"Let's do it." He donned his helmet then, on his way out the door, snagged a long pry bar he'd use for testing any suspicious areas.

A stout north wind blew against them as they crossed the grounds to the portal that led into the mine. He didn't care, though. He could use the jolt.

"You feelin' okay?" Gravel crunched beneath Ted's steel-toed boots.

"Not particularly."

"Would it have something to do with Celeste?"

"Not anymore, it doesn't." Gage eyed the snow-capped peaks, noting the gray clouds that had begun to settle into the area. It would snow soon.

"What is that supposed to mean?"

"Celeste isn't a part of my life anymore."

His friend studied him as they walked. "You say that as though it's a good thing."

"Trust me, it is."

"So when's your brain going to tell your heart?"

"What?" He looked at Ted.

"You may be giving me the facts, but those dark circles under your eyes and the woebegone look on your face have heartache written all over them."

Gage took a deep breath, willing the cool air to clear the fog from his brain. "Sometimes doing the right thing isn't easy."

"What makes you think Celeste exiting your life is a good thing?"

"Ted, there are some things you just know." He stepped through the portal.

"True. However, sometimes fear holds us back from going after what is right."

"What are you? The company psychologist?"

Ted flipped on his headlamp. "I'm just lookin' out for you, my friend."

"Yeah, well, you keep pushing and I might have to move you off of that friend list." He wasn't ready to tell anybody what a loser he was when it came to women. Apparently the only thing he had a talent for was falling in love with the wrong ones.

"Hold on." Pausing, he turned to one of the other miners who was jotting something on a clipboard. "Hey, Wilson."

The older man looked up.

"We're heading down to inspect that new drift." No one went anywhere in a mine without someone else knowing where the person would be.

The man noted the time on his watch and sent them a thumbs-up.

Moving through a series of tunnels and shafts, Gage and Ted continued almost a mile into the mountain, until they reached the drift in question. Average in size, the ceiling stopped at about twelve feet, while the diameter spread to twenty.

Gage pointed to the left with his light. "You start there, I'll work over here."

From the roof to the sides, they'd need to examine every inch of the white quartz for even the slightest of cracks, using their pry bars to test anything in question. A solid ring meant the rock was good, while a drummy thud indicated it was loose.

Working methodically, he was able to focus on the task at hand instead of Celeste, marking unsound areas with spray paint as he went. It felt good to be doing what he loved again. Being inside the mine always energized him. Perhaps it was the anticipation of finding the mother lode or maybe that he'd read Jules Verne's *Journey to the Center of the Earth* one too many times. Whatever the case, today the mine offered him solace.

"I think they made a good move going deep like this." Ted aimed his light against the wall. "Come look at this vein."

Gage joined his friend at the far end of the room. "Oh, yeah." He traced the jagged line along the rocky surface with his flashlight. "This is a nice one. Silver, copper, maybe a little go—"

A loud crack rent the air just then, followed by the sound of thunder and a rush of air.

Turning, Gage instinctively ducked as he watched the ceiling crumble before them. Rocks pelted him.

He yanked Ted against the back wall.

Dust filled the air.

Gage's heart slammed against his rib cage. Sweat beaded his brow. He pressed against the wall as the relentless pounding reverberated around them.

They were going to be buried alive.

Chapter Fifteen

Celeste wandered the empty dining room, disinfecting tables and trying to behave as though all was right with the world. In reality, she hadn't been this miserable since the weeks following her abortion. That hollow feeling that accompanied great loss was something she hadn't ever wanted to feel again. Now it had returned—threefold.

The loss of Gage also meant the loss of his daughters. How had she allowed them to worm their way into her heart in such a short time? But, oh, how she loved having them there.

The way Cassidy and Emma would call her name in unison was a thrill she'd never experienced before. And one she'd likely never experience again.

How could she remain in Ouray, live across the street from the only man she'd ever trusted and those two precious girls, all the while wondering what might have been?

Perhaps her mother was right. Perhaps she should go back to Texas, back to corporate life. Sure, it was stressful, but at least her heart was safe.

Retreating to the kitchen, she lifted the lid on a large pot of chili and stirred the bubbling red mixture. She understood his fierce protectiveness of his daughters. But for him to even think her capable of walking away from them like their mother had hurt her most of all. Yes, she'd done a foolish thing. Selfish even. But she also knew the sting of abandonment.

Get over it, Celeste. A month ago you couldn't even stand the guy.

That's right.

She replaced the lid. How could she possibly be in love with Gage? Infatuated, perhaps. Maybe it wasn't him at all. Maybe it was the girls who'd occupied such a big part of her heart.

She recalled the way he looked at her that day she almost fell off the ladder. And then that same look just before he'd kissed her in the mine. He made her feel special. Protected.

Loved.

She heaved out a sigh. She loved him, all right.

Now she'd have to find a way to move past it.

No use crying over spilt milk, Granny would say.

"Cookie dough is in the fridge." Leslie, her newest waitress, appeared from the storeroom carrying a box of individually packaged crackers.

"Thanks, Leslie. I appreciate you taking care of that for me." Normally Celeste loved making her trademark cookies, but today, she didn't have the heart for it.

Voices echoed from the direction of the front door, so she quickly washed her hands and returned to the dining room. She seated her guests, took their drink orders, then headed for the coffeepot, willing herself to focus on something besides Gage.

One way she could do that was to start looking for a new contractor. Since the demolition was complete, perhaps one of those guys who had frowned on the idea of salvaging would be more accepting now. Though she doubted they'd have Gage's attention to detail.

She delivered the two mugs of coffee and pulled out her order pad. "Are you ready to order?"

The town whistle cut through the air just then. The whistle went off every day at noon and whenever there was an emergency.

She glanced at her watch. Ten fifty-nine.

The sound of multiple sirens echoed throughout the town and she, along with her waitress and two guests, stared out the front window to see what was going on.

A pickup truck and a Jeep SUV practically flew down Main Street with their emergency lights flashing. Something big had happened, that's for sure. An accident on the highway, perhaps.

Closing her eyes, she sent up a quick prayer for all involved.

The door flew open then and Karla rushed inside. "Celeste…" She hurried toward her, seemingly out of breath. "I just came from the bank. There's been an accident at the mine."

Thoughts of Gage filled Celeste's mind. "Which mine?"

"The Golden Girl."

Celeste's heart dropped to her feet.

She swallowed hard. "What kind of accident?"

"I'm not sure. But there were an awful lot of rescue personnel headed that way."

God, please let Gage be okay. As well as everyone else.

She drew in a bolstering breath. Gage was fine. She had to believe that. However, she couldn't sit back and do nothing.

Her mother stormed into the restaurant. "Anybody know what's going on with all of the sirens?"

"Yes, Mom. There's been an accident at the mine."

"*The* mine?"

Celeste knew what her mother was thinking. "Yes, the Golden Girl."

Refusing to give in to the mounting tension, she gathered the rampant thoughts that were trying hard to overtake her common sense and tossed them into a darkened corner of her mind.

"All right. Those emergency workers are going to need food. Karla, are you able to stay?"

"I was hoping you'd ask."

"Good. I've got a pot of chili on the stove. We'll take that."

"There's leftover roast beef and smoked turkey breast in the refrigerator," said Karla. "Why don't I slice them for sandwiches?"

"Perfect." Celeste paused. "Wait. My bread order isn't due until later today." She turned to her mother. "I need you run to Duckett's Market and get me every loaf of white or whole wheat bread you can find."

"How about some fruits and vegetables?" her mother asked.

"Most of these people are men, Mom. They need hearty food."

"Apples and bananas make a filling snack."

"Okay, fine. Get some bananas and apples. Just hurry."

With that, her mother was out the door.

While Leslie covered the dining room, Celeste set to work with Karla in the kitchen. By the time her mother returned with the bread, the meat was sliced and they'd set up an assembly line with everything else they'd need.

Celeste tore open two loaves and began putting together sandwiches. "One more thing, Mom. I need to borrow your vehicle."

"Whatever for?"

"Because it's a four-wheel drive. My Mustang won't make it up the mountain."

"All right. I'll go get it."

Thirty minutes later, Celeste, Karla and Hillary were loading up the back of the SUV. The chili and sandwiches had been placed in large coolers and there was a basket with apples and bananas. A box of chips and a tray of cookies rounded out the offerings, along with disposable bowls, utensils and napkins.

"Please, be careful," her mother said as Celeste closed the hatch. "I don't want those rescue people having to rescue you."

"Don't worry, Mom." She hugged her. "Will you do me one more favor?"

"Of course, darling."

"Will you manage the restaurant while I'm gone?" She waited for the cringe, wince or some other indication that her mother loathed the idea.

Instead, the woman smiled. "I'd be happy to."

Relieved, Celeste headed south of town and maneuvered her mother's rental up the county road that led to the mine. But when the road narrowed and she found herself navigating winding curves that were no more than one-car-width wide and bordered by a wall of rock on one side and a sheer drop-off on the other, her anxiety heightened. To think, people actually did this for fun.

Since she hadn't driven up here before, she wasn't sure how far the mine was. She only knew that it would be impossible to miss.

Again, her thoughts drifted to Gage. Yet instead of dismissing them, she allowed them to linger. *Dear God, please keep him safe. Cassidy and Emma need him so.*

What would she do if she saw him? If he saw her? Would he think she came to check on him?

Ridiculous. She had a trunk full of food. She was there on a mission and that's all there was to it.

Coming off a sharp curve, she spotted a small sea of vehicles, emergency and otherwise, parked to her left. As she drew closer, she saw a wooden bridge with an open gate. Piles of crushed rock flanked the road leading into the compound. A compound that consisted of one very large building and several smaller ones. Though the larger one appeared to extend from the conifer-covered mountainside.

Following the lead of the other cars, she parked beside a large pine tree, exited the SUV and jogged toward a group of people who were clustered outside the larger building. She'd let them know about the food and find out where to leave it.

The frigid wind tossed her ponytail until it beat against her cheek. She cinched the belt on her wool coat and held tight to the collar, grateful that she'd worn her riding boots with the high shaft and low heel today. Walking on layers of crushed rock in heels would have been quite a challenge.

"There's Celeste."

Hearing her name, she scanned the group, her gaze stopping on Gage's mother.

Celeste picked up her pace, noting that his father, Phil, was there, too.

The noose around Celeste's heart tightened. *Please, let Gage be okay. Please, let Gage by okay...*

Bonnie hugged her, long and tight. "I'm so glad you're here. Gage will be happy to see you."

They obviously didn't know about last night.

"Where is he?"

Bonnie released her, keeping hold of her hands. Only then did Celeste notice her red-rimmed eyes. "You mean you don't know?"

"I was just bringing some food for the rescue workers." She pointed toward her vehicle.

Phil stepped closer, laid a hand on her shoulder. "There's been a cave-in, Celeste. Two people are missing. Gage is one of them."

Over the past few hours, Gage's emotions had gone from panic to frustration to anger and, finally acceptance. There really was nothing they could do but pray and wait for help from the other side. If he and Ted attempted to dig through the rocky mass that blocked their passage, they might find themselves in worse shape than they were now.

Instead, they remained in a fifteen-by-twenty-foot space, surrounded by eerie silence. Sounds he usually took for granted were now conspicuously absent—mechanical noises, the wind rustling through the trees, birds chirping and children playing. Things you normally don't think about. Until they're gone.

He picked up a rock shard and tossed it across the space. "What do you think's going on out there?"

"Oh, I'm sure there's a bunch of people here by now." Ted sat on the floor, leaning against the wall, his arms folded across his chest. "Rescue workers and mine people are strategizing the best way to get to us."

"They don't even know if we're dead or alive."

"You know the rules, Gage. They're going to assume we're alive until they have proof otherwise."

"True." Gage drew his knees in the air and rested his forearms on them. "I wonder if our families are out there." He imagined his mother sick with worry, while his father reminded her that God had it all under control. Something Gage could stand to be reminded of, too.

"Probably. Sure wish I had some way to let Laura know I'm okay." Since the drift they were working was new, lines for mine phones hadn't been run yet. And cell phones didn't get reception until you were almost to town.

"I hope somebody remembers to pick my girls up from school." Though how his mother or someone else would explain his absence to Cassidy and Emma remained a mystery. He could only pray that whoever it was would put a positive spin on things. He didn't even want to think about how his girls would react if they feared for one second that they might never see him again.

Thoughts of Celeste crept into his mind. She was one of those people who'd always been good at putting things in a positive light. He was still in awe of how she was able to thwart Emma's tantrums. Even when disciplining the girls, Celeste found a way to make them obey without raising her voice or making them feel as though they were in trouble.

But she wasn't a part of their lives anymore. He straightened. The girls' well-being was far more important than his wish for a wife and helpmate, right? Celeste was used to looking out for number one. Just like the girls' mother.

"You know—" Ted started and Gage welcomed the distraction "—when we were kids, we would have thought it was the coolest thing in the world to be trapped in a mine."

"Are you kidding? I used to pray for it."

"Well, then, looks like God answered your prayers."

Gage chuckled. "Yeah. You know what they say. Sometimes He says yes, sometimes He says wait. Guess I never figured I'd have to wait this long."

"That's why they also say, be careful what you pray for." Ted shifted against the rocky wall. "I hate to bring this up, but we might want to consider dousing our lights for a while. No telling how long we'll be in here. I know these LED things don't use as much power. Still, if we're talking days…"

"I hear ya, man. I don't like it, but I hear you."

Gage reached for his lamp, as did Ted.

Surrounded by the darkest blackness he'd ever known, Gage's thoughts returned first to his girls, then, even though he knew he shouldn't, to Celeste. What would she do when she found out he was trapped? Would she be sad? Would she worry?

Yes to all of the above. But more important, she'd pray. Regardless of how he'd treated her, she would pray for his safety and for his girls.

Why did that seem like such a revelation?

Because Tracy wasn't the praying kind. A worrier, yes. Prayer warrior, no.

Celeste isn't Tracy.

Despite the silence, that small, still voice seemed to grow louder.

What are You trying to tell me, God?

"So what happened between you and Celeste?"

In the darkness, it was as though God had spoken to him. Except he doubted that God had Ted's voice.

Now he had to figure out how to respond. He could ignore the question, but he knew Ted well enough to know he'd keep asking until he got some answers. Considering they'd probably be stuck together for a long while, he may as well throw his friend a bone.

"I learned something about her—about her past—that caused me to rethink our relationship."

"Ah, yes, the dreaded past. Last time I checked, you have one of those, too, Gage."

"You're hilarious, Beatty."

"No, I'm actually quite serious. I mean, are you the same person you were five or ten years ago?"

Gage chuckled. It had been only nine years ago that he and Tracy married. He'd never forget the way she stressed over that wedding. Everything had to be perfect. The thing was so big and lavish, you would have thought they were royalty.

Unfortunately, her quest for perfection didn't stop with their wedding. Tracy had to have the perfect house, the perfect job, the perfect car...

Then Cassidy came along and he soon realized that a child didn't fit into Tracy's perfect plans. Plans that placed a higher value on career than children.

He shook his head. "No, I'm not." He'd like to think he was wiser. Definitely more cautious.

"So what makes you think Celeste is?"

"Ted, I know what you're trying to do here, man, but things aren't that simple. Protecting Cassidy and Emma is my first priority."

"You think Celeste is going to hurt them?"

"Not physically, no."

"But emotionally."

Gage rubbed his palms on his jeans, feeling the dusty grit beneath his fingers. "It's possible. I mean, they're Tracy's flesh and blood and that didn't stop her."

Ted was silent for a moment. Then he said, "I have no doubt that Cassidy and Emma were hurt when their mother left. But I'm not convinced that this breakup with Celeste is entirely about them."

"I've told you, man, the girls are priority number one. I love Celeste. So if it wasn't about Cassidy and Emma, what possible reason would I have for breaking up with her?"

"Because *you're* afraid of getting hurt again."

The words hit Gage like a sledgehammer. Ted was way off base. Gage longed to argue that it wasn't true, but the words refused to come.

Swallowing his pride, he tilted his head upward. *Lord, is that what I'm doing? Using my daughters as an excuse?*

"Think about it, Gage. What if God put Celeste in your life to be the mother I know you want your girls to have?"

Chapter Sixteen

Missing?

That could mean Gage was...

No. Celeste refused to even think it.

White-knuckling the steering wheel, she drove her mother's rented SUV down the mountain, willing the tears that stung the backs of her eyes to go away. Maneuvering these switchbacks was difficult enough without blurred vision.

Besides, she'd told Bonnie she would pick Cassidy and Emma up from school, and she needed to be strong for them. Gage would be okay. She had to believe that. If for nothing more than her own sanity.

Apparently her faith wasn't strong enough, though, as every worst-case scenario shot through her mind. Only one way to remedy that.

"Jesus, Jesus, Jesus, sweetest name I know..." She sang it loud and proud, just like Granny taught her, all the way back into town, slaying the dreadful images that threatened to drag her under.

Her faith was bolstered and the tears banished. That is, until she stepped into Granny's Kitchen.

"Well?" Her mother rounded the counter.

"Mission accomplished." She removed her wool pea-coat and started toward the kitchen. "I dropped off the food and they were most appreciative."

"They who?" Karla was right on her heels.

"The workers, of course." She was avoiding the inevitable and she knew it. They wanted details about the accident but, despite her little praise-and-worship session in the car, she found herself not wanting to deliver the news about Gage. Because she might fall apart doing so.

Her mother took hold of her elbow, stopping Celeste's retreat. "What did you learn about the accident?"

She draped the coat over her arm, refusing to look at either woman. "There was a cave-in. Two men are missing." She took a shaky breath. "One of them is Gage."

Karla's hand flew to her mouth. Not exactly what Celeste needed right now.

Her mother continued to study her. "Do they know if they're alive?"

Celeste shook her head. "Not yet." She checked the time on her watch. Two twenty. "I promised Bonnie I would get the girls from school." She again focused on her coat, removing imaginary signs of lint from the dark brown wool. "I'd prefer not to bring them here. If they overheard someone talking—" She shrugged. "So I'm going to close the restaurant early today."

"Nonsense." Her mother waved a hand. "I can handle dinner and closing."

Celeste couldn't have been more shocked if Gage walked through the door at that very moment. Twice in one day her mother had agreed to work the restaurant. This time she'd even volunteered.

"Are you sure?" she asked her mother.

"You forget I used to work in this restaurant as a teen."

"I'll stay, too." Karla dabbed at her eyes. "Make sure *she* stays out of trouble."

"Trouble?" Her mother dug her fists into her hips. "You're the one who used to get into trouble. Why, I remember when you and Rosemary Hiccum—"

"Wait a minute." Celeste held up a hand, trying to piece things together. "You two know each other?"

Karla poked a thumb in Hillary's direction. "Sat beside her in just about every class from kindergarten all the way through graduation."

Celeste's gaze moved from her mother to Karla and back again. The two women were so different that it hadn't dawned on her that they were likely the same age. Sometimes she even forgot that her mother had grown up here.

She laid a hand to the side of her face. "Well, if that don't beat all."

With assurances that tonight's special was already in the oven, Celeste shrugged back into her coat, exited the restaurant and started in the direction of the school. A brisk northerly wind had her tugging the fur-lined leather gloves from her pockets and making her wish she'd opted to drive. Hopefully the girls had warm coats. Either way, hot chocolate would definitely be in order when they got back to the condo.

Outside the beige brick building that housed every grade from pre-K through twelve, Emma was the first to spot Celeste. And the smile that exploded on her face brightened Celeste's somber mood.

"Hello, sweet girl." Celeste knelt to greet her.

Emma charged toward Celeste, her pink Barbie backpack and the pom-pom on her knit cap bouncing with every step, until she threw herself into Celeste's waiting arms.

When Cassidy found Celeste a couple of minutes later, her smile was just as big.

Celeste gave her a hug. "How was your day?" She brushed the hair away from Cassidy's face.

"Good." The girl cocked her head to peer up at Celeste. "How come you're picking us up?"

"Well—" she couldn't tell them the whole truth, so she'd have to settle for part of it "—your daddy had to stay late at the mine and your grandmother was busy." She took hold of both their mitten-clad hands. "So I get to have you girls all to myself."

"Yay!" Emma cheered.

Celeste turned toward Cassidy. "Do you have any homework?"

The child shook her head.

"Well, all right. Looks like we get to play."

"Play?" A curious smile lit both their faces.

Out of the corner of her eye, Celeste saw Jan Fincher heading toward them. Cassidy's friend Bella's mom. And from the woeful look on Jan's face, Celeste knew what she was about to say. Ouray was a small town and news traveled fast, so even if she didn't know that it was Gage who was missing, she knew about the accident.

"I'm so sorry to hear—"

Taking a step back from the girls so they wouldn't see her, Celeste subtly shook her head and mouthed the word *No*, her gaze falling to the girls. She was relieved when Bella's mother acknowledged her efforts with a nod.

Celeste resumed her position between the girls, suddenly glad that tomorrow was Saturday and there would be no school. "Yes, Gage has to spend some extra time up at the mine, so the girls are coming home with me."

Jan forced a smile as she addressed the girls. "Oh, I'm sure you'll have lots of fun with Celeste."

"Uh-huh." Emma nodded emphatically.

"We always have fun with Celeste." The smile Cassidy sent Celeste kept her warm all the way down Eighth Avenue and back to her condo.

"How come we didn't go to Granny's Kitchen?" Cassidy dropped her backpack at the top of the stairs.

Good question. When Gage was still working on the suites, he'd pick them up then leave them with her in the restaurant. Of course, today she had one very good reason for not wanting them there. Not that she could share it with them.

"I thought it would be more fun to hang out here." Celeste grabbed a saucepan from the cupboard, then retrieved the milk from the refrigerator. "Anyone up for some hot chocolate?"

"Me!" they said in unison.

"Do you have any cookies?" Emma peered hopefully up at her.

"Sorry, sweetie." Before Emma could frown, Celeste added, "But we can make some."

That earned another round of cheers.

Two hours later, the girls were coloring at the table while Celeste worked on dinner. Keeping the girls had not only been the right thing to do, but a good thing. Kept her from dwelling on Gage and what was happening at the mine.

She had just put a pan of oven-baked chicken into the oven when she heard her cell ring.

Glancing at the screen, she saw Taryn's name and froze. Sure, she could be calling about the girls, but what if there was news on Gage? Bad news? Either way, she'd never know until she answered.

"Hi, Taryn."

The girls' heads popped up briefly.

"Hey, Celeste." Taryn sounded weary. That mix of worry and uncertainty no doubt dragging her down.

She turned her back to the girls and cupped her hand around the phone. "Any word?"

"No. Sorry. I do need to ask a favor, though."

"Sure." Celeste double-checked the oven temp and eyed the girls.

"Do you suppose you could keep Cassidy and Emma tonight? Dad wants to try to get Mom home for a few hours of rest later, but she's going to want someone from the family to be at the mine in case anything happens. My brother, Randy, and I are going to take turns."

Celeste knew exactly how Bonnie felt. She hadn't wanted to leave either. However, she no longer had a right to be there. Besides, it was better this way. The girls needed someone to take care of them and she was honored to do it.

"No need to explain, Taryn. I'd love to keep the girls."

"You have been such a blessing to them, Celeste. To all of us."

Celeste blinked away the unbidden tears and glanced at the sweet faces around her table. "Trust me, I'm getting my fair share of blessings, too."

"I'll be by in a little bit to drop off some of their things."

"Sounds great. We'll see you then."

"Do we have to go to Aunt Tawyn's?" Emma said as Celeste put down the phone.

"Sorry, girls. It looks like you're going to have to stay with me tonight."

The two looked at each other, their surprise morphing into delighted smiles.

"All right!" They high-fived each other.

Gage might not be happy when he found out she had

kept his girls, but tonight that didn't matter. They needed her as much as she needed them. Together, they would weather this storm.

Gage wondered what his girls were doing. Where they were? Whom were they with? Were they wondering where he was?

He'd always known the dangers of working in a mine. That every time he went inside he was putting his life at risk. Yet, somehow, that knowledge had never really sunk in. Until now.

He was grateful to be alive. But he was also hungry, thirsty and tired, despite drifting in and out of sleep for the past who knew how many hours. A bed of rock wasn't the most comfortable resting spot.

Using the wall as his guide, he pushed to his feet and stretched.

All of this uncertainty was about to drive him crazy. They'd heard faint noises from the other side, but nothing they could pinpoint. He wished they'd work faster. Then again, there was no telling how far up the drift the cave-in had gone. Could be ten feet, could be a hundred.

He only knew that he needed to get out of here so he could make things right with Celeste. Ted was right. Her past needed to remain where it was—in the past. Right along with Gage's and all the foolish mistakes he'd made.

She'd learned to stand up to her mother by not only moving to Ouray, but in her refusal to leave. And it would be impossible for him to ignore the caring, nurturing manner in which she interacted with his daughters. Instinctively doing those motherly things he so desperately wanted for Cassidy and Emma. Like slaying the tickle monster.

That, along with so many memories, made him smile.

Like when he'd kissed her inside the Bachelor-Syracuse. It was then that he'd asked if she trusted him. She had. And she'd trusted him enough to share something that was obviously very personal and painful for her.

What did he do?

He reacted. Reacted without talking to God. Reacted without taking Celeste's feelings into consideration. Instead, he turned his back on her. Just as Tracy had done to him and Celeste's father had done to her.

He acted like a grade-A, first-class jerk. One who seriously needed to apologize. Needed her to know that he still loved her and that her past didn't matter.

He slumped against the wall. Who was he kidding? As if that was going to fix everything. Just because he said he was sorry didn't mean she'd be ready to forgive and pick up where they left off. Celeste was a strong woman. One who was comfortable in her own skin and content to be single. She might just tell him to take his stupid apology and go pound sand.

After the blow he dealt her, he couldn't say he'd blame her.

Ignoring the darkness, he closed his eyes and bowed his head.

Lord, I need Your help in so many ways. Thank You for protecting Ted and me from the collapse. Please watch over Cassidy and Emma and guide the rescuers as they work to get to us. Be with my family and Ted's. Give them peace and, somehow, let them know that we're okay.

He drew in a breath. *About Celeste, Lord...Your ways are higher than my ways. I never planned to fall in love again, yet it happened anyway. Now I've messed it up. Is Celeste a part of Your plan for my life? I pray so. But even if it's not, I ask that You would allow me to make things right with her. That we could at least be friends and she'd still be a part of my daughters' lives.*

"Gage?" Ted sounded as weary as he was.

"Yeah?"

"Do you hear that?"

Gage listened. For the first time since the cave-in, he actually heard something. "Sounds mechanical."

"Yeah, like a mucking machine." Ted turned on his flashlight and smiled in Gage's direction. "You know what that means? They're comin' after us."

Chapter Seventeen

Saturday morning presented Celeste with a new set of challenges. Since Karla had a prior commitment and Celeste had already promised two other members of her waitstaff they could have the day off, it appeared that she'd have to bring Cassidy and Emma with her to Granny's Kitchen.

The girls wouldn't mind. They loved it there. But Celeste still worried that they might overhear something about the accident at the mine. And protecting them was her number-one priority. On that point, she and Gage would agree.

So with a prayer on her lips and little more than three hours of sleep, Celeste had gone to the restaurant early to get the cinnamon rolls ready. Cassidy and Emma had crawled into bed and were asleep before nine last night, but slumber had eluded Celeste. Images of Gage, both good and bad, plagued her with every toss and turn. So she prayed there would be some word on him today.

With the cinnamon rolls rising and icing waiting in the fridge, she returned to her condo in the predawn darkness to trade places with her mother. Hillary had once again surprised her by offering to open the restaurant while Celeste waited for the girls to wake up. Celeste was even starting to get the feeling that her mother actually enjoyed helping out at Granny's Kitchen.

God had been working a lot of miracles where her mother was concerned. Now she prayed He would work one for Gage and Ted.

Emma was the first to awake. Coffee cup in hand, Celeste looked up from her Bible as Emma padded down the stairs in her Hello Kitty pajamas, dragging her unicorn blanket. She smiled when she saw Celeste and quickened her pace.

"Good morning, sweet girl." She set her mug on the side table and welcomed the child into her lap.

"Good morning." She snuggled against Celeste, laying her head against her shoulder.

Celeste covered her with the blanket. "Are you warm enough?"

Emma nodded.

They sat quietly. Something Celeste knew would change once Emma was fully awake. So she rested her cheek against Emma's head and watched out the window as the sun backlit the peaks of the Amphitheater, savoring these few precious moments. How she would love to start every day this way.

She closed her eyes, trying to banish the thought. Gage had made it clear that whatever was between them was over. Hard to believe that the love he proclaimed to have for her could die in an instant. Perhaps it wasn't love after all.

Her hold tightened on Emma. What would happen to these precious girls if Gage didn't make it out?

His family would likely take them. Maybe Taryn or her other brother would raise them. But the thought of Cassidy and Emma growing up without their father or their mother broke Celeste's heart. They'd already suffered such loss.

God, please bring Gage back to them.

A few minutes later, Cassidy awoke and when the girls found out they'd be spending the day at Granny's Kitchen, they couldn't get ready fast enough. By eight forty-five, they were settled at the restaurant's counter, devouring scrambled eggs and sausage like they hadn't eaten in a week.

"Would you two sugar muffins like to split a cinnamon roll?"

Celeste turned from the coffeemaker, pot in hand, and stared at her mother. Sugar muffins? Where had that come from?

As lunchtime approached, the number of guests swelled as television crews poured into town to cover the mine accident. Between kitchen duty and waiting tables, Celeste and her mother were busier than a one-legged grasshopper in a jumping contest. Fortunately, Cassidy and Emma were quite content with the salt dough Celeste had made for them. They sat at the counter, armed with cookie cutters and rolling pins, letting their imaginations run wild.

Celeste set a double-deluxe burger and fries in front of a man not much older than her.

He looked up at her, his expression intense. "Miss, do you know either of the men who are missing?"

Surprised by his question, she pulled from her corporate past for a response. "Ouray is a small town. Everyone is familiar."

"Do you believe they'll find Mr. Purcell and Mr. Beatty alive?" If his first question surprised her, this one infuriated her.

She squared her shoulders. "Faith is all we have, sir. Without it, we're lost."

Turning on her heel, she headed across the dining room and through the kitchen and fell against the wall in her office as grief finally got the best of her. Sobs racked her body and she had to clasp a hand over her mouth to prevent them from escaping.

God, please, please, please let Gage be alive. Take me in his place if You have to. Just bring Gage back for his daughters.

"Celeste?"

She opened her eyes to find her mother standing before her.

"I was wondering when this was going to catch up with you." Mom smoothed a hand across Celeste's hair. "You love him, don't you?"

Lowering her hand, she nodded.

"Then you should be up at the mine. I can take care of the girls."

"If only it were that simple." She snagged a tissue from the box on her desk. "I can't go into it now, but Gage broke things off the other night." She could see the questions in her mother's eyes. "The best thing I can do now is take care of his girls."

"Celeste?" The child's voice trembled.

"Cassidy?" She looked down to see both girls standing in the doorway of her office, their big blue eyes swimming with unshed tears. "What is it, sweetheart?" She knelt, laying a hand on each of their arms.

"What happened to Daddy?" Cassidy's bottom lip quivered.

Celeste glanced at her mother, then back to the girls. *Dear, God. Help me.*

"What do you mean, sugar?" Her mother managed the words first.

"We heard some man talking on the phone." A tear slipped onto Cassidy's cheek. "He said there were two men missing and then I heard my daddy's name." The child fell into Celeste's embrace, weeping.

Celeste cringed. This was her fault for leaving them alone.

She held out her other arm to Emma, who was also crying, then set her bottom on the tile floor and held them in her lap. She stroked their hair as her mother had done with her just moments before. Now it was time for her to take on that role. If only for this moment.

She looked up at her mother. "We'll be okay."

With a parting kiss atop Celeste's head, her mother left them.

Celeste gathered her flailing emotions as an inexplicable peace fell over her.

"It's true. There was an accident at the mine and your daddy is missing." She felt their bodies tense, heard their gentle cries. She pulled them closer. "So we have to pray very hard, and believe, that your daddy will be okay."

"But what if he isn't?" Cassidy sniffed. "What if he goes away like our mommy did?"

Celeste's heart wrenched. *God, I can't do this. You have to help me. Give me Your words.*

"Well, I don't know. But I do know that God will never leave us. We simply have to trust Him to make everything okay." She rubbed their arms, understanding all too well the turmoil going on inside them.

God can use those bad things in our lives to help somebody else. She could hear her grandmother's words as though she were sitting right beside her. And if there was even a morsel of her story that could help Cassidy and Emma…

"You know, girls, my daddy went away when I was a little girl."

Surprise lit their sad faces.

"What did you do?" asked Cassidy.

"At first, I was very sad."

"For how long?" asked Emma.

"For a long time. Even though I still had my mom and my granny, I missed my daddy something fierce."

"Do you still miss him?" Cassidy relaxed against her.

"Sometimes. But it doesn't hurt anymore."

"Why not?"

"Well, one day my heart was hurting so bad I thought it might explode. So I talked to God—matter of fact, I think I might have even yelled—and told Him exactly how I felt. I wasn't just sad, I was mad."

Cassidy gasped. "Did you tell Him that, too?"

"I did." Her gaze darted between the two. "I told Him that I didn't want my heart to hurt anymore and that He was the only one who could fix it."

"What happened?" Curiosity had replaced some of Cassidy's tears.

"He fixed it. Not right away, but over time the hurt went away."

They continued to watch her.

"The Bible tells us that we do not have because we do not ask God."

Emma popped her head up. "Does that mean I can ask Him for a pony?"

Celeste breathed out a chuckle. "No."

"Then what does it mean?" asked Cassidy.

"It means that when we're hurting or when we're in need—" she glanced at Emma "—which is different than a want—" she turned back to Cassidy "—all we have to do is ask God to help us."

She hugged them once again. "I love you girls so much."

"We love you, too," said Cassidy.

"Will you be our mommy?" Emma's expression had never been more serious.

Celeste blinked, barely able to speak around the lump in her throat. "Sweetheart, I would love to be your mommy. But, right now, we need to concentrate on your daddy and ask God to bring him back to us."

"Will you pray, too?" asked Cassidy.

If she never held these precious girls again and Gage was nothing more than her friend, they would always be in her prayers. "You can count on it."

Fifty hours after their ordeal began, Gage and Ted emerged from the mine to the cheers of rescue workers, townspeople, family and friends.

Gage squinted against the gray skies and breathed in the pristine snowy air, his heart filled with gratitude and anticipation.

"Daddy!"

The sight of his girls running toward him, ponytails flying and smiles as big as he'd ever seen, lodged a mountain of a boulder in his throat. He knelt to greet them, and the force of their little bodies slamming into his nearly toppled him. He didn't care, though. They were here. Together. A family once again.

"Why are you crying, Daddy?" asked Emma.

He hadn't even noticed the tears. "Because I'm so happy to see you." He squeezed them tighter.

Cassidy's giggle sounded like the sweetest music he'd ever heard. "You're prickly." She rubbed the stubble lining his jaw.

"And dirty." Emma patted his shirt, sending puffs of dust into the air.

"Things got a little messy in there."

"I missed you, Daddy." Emma kissed his cheek. "But Celeste takeded good care of us."

"She did?" Looking beyond his daughters, he scanned the row of family members. Each and every one of them was there. Except for the one person he really wanted—needed—to see.

"Uh-huh." Cassidy nodded. "We prayed for you and she taught us that even if something bad happened, God would never leave us."

"Oh, yeah?" He struggled to stand, his gaze drifting to his mother, who was awaiting her own hug.

"The girls have been with Celeste this entire time." She wrapped her arms around him, laying her head against his chest. "I'm so glad you're okay." He could feel her tears seeping through his shirt.

"So am I, Mom. So am I." Releasing her, he again searched the faces. His brother, Randy, was there along with Amanda and their son. Cash was with Taryn. His father. "Where's Celeste?"

"She refused to come." Taryn shrugged. "Said it wasn't her place to be here."

His heart sank.

He let go a sigh, his breath visible in the chilly air. "That would be my fault."

Taryn crossed her arms over her chest and glared. "Gage Purcell, what did you do? Celeste is the best thing that ever happened to you."

"I realize that now." Unfortunately, it might be too late. He'd taken her trust and thrown it back in her face. And he wasn't sure he'd ever be able to earn it back. But he was determined to try.

The hugs continued until the rescue people came and urged him into the ambulance. They transported him to the hospital in Montrose for a once-over where, aside from tending a few scrapes and cuts, they gave him a round of IV fluids, then sent him home.

Darkness had fallen by the time he and his parents returned to Ouray. He didn't care, though. He was just grateful to be home.

Inside, the rest of his family welcomed him.

"Daddy, you gotta come see." Cassidy tugged his hand and led him into the kitchen, where a melody of aromas captured his attention, making his stomach growl with vengeance.

"What's going on?"

Taryn and Amanda stepped away from the stove.

"Food." Taryn motioned to the counter. "And lots of it."

His gaze traveled the virtual buffet of foil-covered pans lining his counter. "Looks like the women of Ouray have outdone themselves."

"I would say so." Amanda lifted the lid on a pot and gave the contents a stir. "We've got everything from enchiladas to soup to lasagna."

"Enchiladas?"

"Yes, sir." His sister-in-law nodded. "Celeste brought them, along with two pans of cinnamon rolls."

That was so like her to remember his favorites. And the fact that she'd cared for his daughters, guiding them through what had to have been a difficult time, only confirmed that she was the perfect mother for them and the perfect woman for him.

After dinner, Gage felt as though he were about to collapse. His family must have gotten the hint, because once the kitchen was clean, they all left. Now if he could just get his daughters into bed.

"But Daddy, I need my unicorn blankie."

"Where did you have it last?"

"At Celeste's."

Naturally. Yet for as eager as he was to see Celeste, he wasn't exactly keen on doing it now. He was exhausted. On the other hand, if he didn't retrieve the blanket, Emma would never go to sleep. At least not without a great deal of effort on his part.

Which meant he had no other choice.

Boy, was this going to be awkward.

"All right, Emma. I'll get your blanket. Your job—" he poked her belly with his finger "—is to brush your teeth and get into bed. Do you think you can do that?"

She wrapped her little arms around his hips and squeezed. "Uh-huh."

"Okay." He patted her. "I'll be right back."

He stepped into the cold night air and made his way down the steps. Apparently the snow had been confined to the higher elevations, because there were no signs of any around town.

Noting the lights in Celeste's living room, he crossed the street, his nerves getting the best of him. The last time he and Celeste had talked, he'd behaved like a jerk. Yet for as much as he longed to talk to her now, to apologize and at least attempt to make things right, this wasn't the time. Exhaustion aside, he needed to get back to the girls.

Still, he needed to say something. He just didn't know what.

A minute later, he rang the bell and waited.

The porch light turned on and Celeste opened the door.

Her sharp intake of breath told him just how surprised she was to see him. She looked shocked, but more beautiful than ever with her hair piled on top of her head and those cute princess pajamas. Just like that night she found the bear in her garage.

"Hi."

"Hi." She held tight to the door handle, as though nervous.

He poked a thumb behind him. "Emma forgot her unicorn blanket."

"Ah. It must not have made it into the bag I gave Taryn." Her smile was shy. "But…you could have called, you know."

"I wasn't sure you'd answer." He jammed his hands into his pockets. "Listen, I, uh, I want to thank you for looking after Cassidy and Emma. No one could have seen them through this as well as you did."

"I was honored to do it." She met his gaze for the first time. "I love them both very much."

Before he could respond, Celeste cleared her throat. "I'll just get that blanket."

Through the crack in the door, he watched her disappear up the stairs. A few moments later, she returned.

"Took me a second to find it." She handed it to him.

"As important as this thing is to her—" he held up the soft fuzzy fabric "—she's apt to leave it just about anywhere."

Celeste's soft laughter warmed him.

He didn't want to leave. Especially with so much left unsaid between them. But what choice did he have?

"I guess I'd better get back. Good night, Celeste." He turned and started down the drive.

"Gage?"

He twisted to see Celeste coming toward him in her bare feet.

She paused a moment before pushing up on her tiptoes to hug him around the neck. "I'm so thankful you're safe." Her words were warm on his ear.

He wanted to hold her. To tell her that he loved her. Before his brain could tell him what to do, though, she was on her way back to the condo, sending him a quick wave before closing the door.

Chapter Eighteen

Monday morning as the sun rose above the Amphitheater, Gage rang Celeste's doorbell, feeling even more nervous than he had last night. He knew Celeste would be at Granny's Kitchen, but he hoped her mother was home.

Hillary opened the door, looking as though she'd just stepped off the pages of a fashion magazine, and stared at him, a mixture of emotions rolling across her face. She opened her mouth to speak, then closed it without saying a word, making him even more anxious.

"Good morning, Hillary. I was wondering if we might be able to talk."

She took a step back, holding the door wide. "Yes, of course."

"Would you care for a cup of coffee?" She spoke over her shoulder as he followed her up the stairs to the living area.

"Coffee would be great. Thank you."

"Have a seat." She motioned to the table before continuing into the kitchen. "We were so relieved to learn that you were okay. I can't imagine how dreadful that must have been for you." She grabbed a mug from the cupboard and filled it. "Cream or sugar?"

"No, thank you."

She replaced the coffeepot and joined him at the table. "They said there was a cave-in. Were you buried?" The concern in her brown eyes surprised him.

"No." He cradled the mug, letting the warmth seep into his cold fingers. "We were trapped in a small pocket."

"Thank the Lord for that. Still—" she lifted her cup "—that had to have been harrowing, not knowing if or when they'd find you. Not to mention just being trapped." She shuddered and took a sip.

"Let's just say it's not something I care to repeat."

"I don't blame you." Another sip, then she set her cup on the table. "So what was it you wanted to talk about?"

"Your daughter."

"I should have guessed that."

"I love her."

"Then why did you tell her you couldn't see her anymore?"

He must have appeared surprised, because she said, "Yes, she told me what happened."

His anxiety ratcheted up a notch.

He stared at the steaming black liquid in his mug. "Sending her away that night was the biggest mistake of my life."

"Then why did you?"

There was no way he could skirt around things. Hillary wouldn't accept anything but the truth. And considering what he was about to ask her, the truth was exactly what she deserved.

"A couple of years ago, my wife walked out on me and the girls." He proceeded to fill Celeste's mother in on some of the details of their relationship and why Tracy had left. "So when Celeste told me about her past—"

"Rather out of character for my daughter, isn't it?"

He looked at her now. "I wasn't sure if you were aware."

"Not until recently." She wrapped her fingers around her cup, her expression worrisome. "And I regret that my actions made her feel that she had no other choice."

"Hey, if there's one thing I've learned, it's that this parenting gig isn't easy. I have no doubt you raised Celeste the best you could."

She sent him a weak smile. "Thank you."

"I'm just speaking the truth."

"I interrupted you."

He shrugged. "In my mind, all I could hear were Tracy's excuses. And I was afraid."

"Gage, I know how it feels to love someone, to trust them. Then to have them turn their back on you. It's a pain no one should have to experience. Unfortunately, I've let the actions of Celeste's father dictate much of my life, because I didn't want to get hurt again."

"It's hard not to when your heart's been trampled on."

"Yes, it is. However, in doing so, we're apt to miss out on something even greater than our pain. Something wonderful." She laid a hand on his arm. "I was trying so hard to make Celeste conform to what I wanted for her, that I was missing out on one of the greatest relationships of my life."

He covered her hand with his. "Your daughter is one of the strongest, most loving and sincere people I've ever known."

Hillary's smile was the biggest he'd ever seen. "Yes, she is."

"Which is why I'd like to ask you for her hand in marriage."

Life in Ouray seemed to be back to normal. At least for most people. Business at Granny's Kitchen had been brisk much of the day, even though the number of reporters had rapidly dwindled, thanks to yesterday's mine rescue.

Celeste, on the other hand, wasn't even sure what normal was anymore. Then again, over the past six weeks there'd been so many changes in her life that she was constantly adjusting to a new norm. And that would be the case again.

She wiped down the coffeemaker, wishing she could rid herself of the ache in her heart. A dull, constant pain brought on by the knowledge that Gage was no longer a part of her life.

Last night when he showed up at her door, she made the mistake of getting her hopes up. Thinking that maybe he was there to apologize and say he wanted her back. A foolish mistake she would not allow herself to make again.

Still, she was grateful for the opportunity to see with her own eyes that he was alive and well, save for that cut over his right eye and a severe case of five o'clock shadow. The mere thought of the alternative made her ill.

The turmoil of these past few days had brought about one very good thing, though. The relationship between her and her mother had not only been strengthened, but had morphed into the kind of close, personal relationship she'd longed for all her life. Mom was Mom, but she was now also Celeste's friend. One she could talk to and share things with, without the fear of reprimand or letting her mother down.

The front door opened.

"I'm sorry, we're clo—" Turning, she saw Gage standing there, clean-shaven and looking way too handsome. "Oh, it's you." She fumbled with her dishrag before dropping it into the bar sink.

He eased toward the counter.

"What can I do for you?"

"Nothing. I just thought I'd walk you home."

Her heart stammered. "Oh. Well, I'm still getting things cleaned up. You don't—"

"I'll wait."

She looked away, uncertain what to say. Funny, she'd never been uncomfortable with Gage before. Back when they were at least friends. At this moment, though, she had no idea where they stood.

"Or better yet—" he rounded the counter "—why don't I help you so you can get out of here sooner."

She took a slow breath, trying to calm her rapid pulse. "Okay."

In no time, she was turning out the lights, while Gage waited by the door.

"All set?" His easy smile sent a wave of awareness dancing through her.

"Yes."

He helped her with her coat, then opened the door.

"Where are the girls?" She locked the door behind her.

"With a sitter."

"Your mother?"

"No. Someone new."

They started down the sidewalk. Strange. She'd never known Gage to use anyone outside his family to watch the girls before. Except for her, that is.

"I wanted to thank you again for looking after Cassidy and Emma. They haven't stopped talking about all the fun they had."

She burrowed her hands in the pockets of her coat. "I did my best to keep things normal. I wanted to protect them from the reality of what was happening up at the mine." She breathed in the chilly night air as they rounded onto Second Street. "Unfortunately, they found out anyway."

"Yes, but you did a good job of helping them deal with the uncertainty and taught them some truths they'll be able to use as they get older."

"I just shared what I knew to be true."

"But you did it in a loving, caring manner. They needed that." He stopped her when they reached her drive. "They needed you."

She looked into those deep blue eyes for what seemed like forever, longing to fall into his embrace and to hear him tell her he loved her just one more time.

But that only happened in fairy tales. Gage may be her Prince Charming, but she was no Cinderella.

"I need to go." She turned for her condo, but he reached for her arm, stopping her retreat.

"Please?" He stepped in front of her. "Can I come inside? I'd like to talk to you."

What on earth could he possibly want to talk to her about? "But, my mother—"

"Is babysitting Cassidy and Emma."

Her gaze jerked to his. "What?"

He shrugged. "They like her. And she likes them. So—" he nodded toward the house "—shall we?"

This was so not a good idea. Even now, she was finding herself more drawn to him than ever. If her heart thought there was even the slightest chance of a reconciliation, she'd be a goner for sure.

That should've stopped her. Instead, she said, "Okay."

Inside, she draped her coat over the back of a dining room chair and gestured for Gage to sit on the couch. Then she made herself as comfortable as she possibly could in the overstuffed chair.

She grabbed the purple throw and laid it across her

legs. "So what did you want to talk about?" The sooner they got this over with, the better off she'd be.

Resting his forearms on his thighs, he rubbed his hands together. "I owe you an apology. I said some very harsh things to you that night at my house."

She looked away, not wanting to see the sincerity in his gaze. "Perhaps. Given what you went through with Tracy, I understand how you would feel that way."

"That's just it, Celeste. You shouldn't have to understand. I never should have said any of that stuff in the first place. You trusted me enough to share something sacred with me. And I used it to hurt you."

She blinked away the sting of tears as he stood and moved toward her.

He knelt in front of her. "I had a lot of time to think inside the mine. And I realized that it wasn't your past that stood in my way, but my own fears." His gaze drifted away, as though he were embarrassed. "The only one I was protecting was me."

"Protecting yourself from what? Me?"

Running a hand through his hair, he looked up at her now. "Yes."

"Why?"

"Because you are a gift." He reached for her hand, intertwining their fingers. "You've brought more joy into my life than I ever imagined possible. And just the thought of losing that scares me more than you can imagine. I love you, Celeste."

The look in those deep blue eyes left no room for doubt. He truly did love her. And she loved him so very much.

He let go of her hand then. "So if you're willing to forgive me—" his hand reappeared, holding a velvet box "—I'd like to spend the rest of my life making it up to you." He opened the box to reveal a beautiful diamond solitaire. "Will you marry me, Celeste? Will you be the mother my daughters deserve?"

Excitement, disbelief and love, so much love, welled inside her. She cradled his handsome face in her hands, the tears she'd been fighting now streaming down her cheeks.

"Love keeps no record of wrongs, Gage. And I do love you, so very much." She kissed his lips. "Yes, I will marry you."

Epilogue

Celeste followed Cassidy and Emma up the Purcells' snow-covered sidewalk, carrying a large basket of slider buns and homemade barbecue sauce. In recent weeks, she'd heard all kinds of stories about Phil and Bonnie's New Year's Eve parties. How they'd been hosting them since their kids were babies and how the parties grew bigger each year. An evening of counting their blessings from the previous year and praying for those that lay ahead.

"Careful, Mom." She glanced over her shoulder. "It's kind of slick up here."

"Did you remember the jalapeños?"

"And the pickles and the onions."

"Good. Because brisket isn't brisket without jalapeños. And I doubt that's something Bonnie keeps in her fridge."

"You'd be correct, Hillary." Gage brought up the rear, holding a large pan of smoked brisket. "Anything hotter than black pepper will have my mom turning up her nose." Coming alongside Celeste, he leaned closer. "Taryn's bringing everything else, right?" he whispered.

"Yes."

"There are my girls." Bonnie held the front door wide

as they climbed the steps of the beautifully restored Victorian house. "Happy New Year, everyone."

Celeste pondered the evergreen garland and tiny white lights that adorned the porch rail. Oh, yes. It was going to be a happy New Year, indeed.

Inside, a mix of popular Christian music and holiday tunes drifted through the air, along with the fragrances of evergreen, cloves and vanilla.

"Everything looks divine, Bonnie." Her mother took off her coat and handed it to their hostess.

The nine-foot Christmas tree still took center stage in the living room, while more greenery and lights adorned doorways, windows and just about any other space that needed sprucing up.

Over the next hour, the house filled with familiar faces, reminding Celeste of the closing scene in *It's a Wonderful Life*. These were the people she had grown to know and love over the past several months.

"Ted!" Gage pushed through the foyer to hug his long-time friend. "So glad you could make it."

"Are you kidding, buddy?" Ted sent Celeste a wink. "I wouldn't miss this for the world."

His wife, Laura, leaned toward Celeste. "We have a lot to be thankful for this year, don't we?"

"We sure do. I don't know what we would have done without them."

"Praise God we didn't have to find out."

Cold air filtered into the room as Trent and Blakely entered with Rose, Austin and Katelynn.

"She's getting so big." Celeste gladly held the baby while Blakely slipped out of her coat.

"Tell me about it." Blakely adjusted the collar of her daughter's pink velvet dress. "She's almost nine pounds."

Cash and Taryn arrived along with his parents and

grandfather, followed by Pastor Dan, his wife, Lisa, and their daughter, Alyssa. The house was bursting at the seams with love, laughter and good food. Just the way Gage and Celeste had envisioned it.

"If I could have everyone's attention." Gage stood on a chair at the entrance to the living room.

Bonnie, Amanda, Taryn and Rose came in from the kitchen.

"Is everybody here?" Gage scanned the adjoining rooms.

"Son—" Bonnie perched a hand on her apron-clad hip "—what on earth are you up to?"

He reached for Celeste's hand. "We've decided to get married."

His mother sent him an annoyed look. "Gage, we all know that. We're just waiting for you to tell us where and when."

He grinned. "Right here. Tonight."

The smile on Bonnie's face right before she let out a squeal that probably echoed throughout the canyon was priceless.

"We've taken care of all the details. All we have to do is get ready," said Gage. "So everyone continue to party and we'll see you shortly."

Stepping down, he kept hold of Celeste's hand and pulled her to him. "Meet me at the altar?"

"I can hardly wait."

Ninety minutes later, Celeste waited at the top of the oak staircase feeling like Cinderella in her cap-sleeve tulle gown. While notes of Beethoven's "Ode to Joy" played in the background, Cassidy and Emma descended first, followed by Celeste's mother, who was also serving as her maid of honor. Smiling guests watched from the living and dining rooms adjacent to the foyer. And at the bottom of the stairs, along with his best man, Ted, and Pastor Dan, was the man Celeste had trusted with her heart. The one she couldn't wait to start a life with and create a happily-ever-after all their own.

They deliberately kept the ceremony short and when the pastor said, "You may kiss your bride," the room erupted with cheers.

A smiling Gage cradled her face and pulled her to him. "Happy New Year, Mrs. Purcell."

"Happy New Year, Mr. Purcell." Filled with more joy and love than she'd ever imagined, she smiled back at her husband. "And many more to come."

* * * * *

Dear Reader,

I hope you enjoyed Gage and Celeste's story, about two people who had planned their lives, yet suddenly found themselves heading in another direction. One they never imagined.

Have you ever done that? Laid out your plans, embarked on your journey through life, were well on your way toward your goal, only to have God set you on another path you hadn't expected? I have. Actually, I suppose I could say that about writing. When my kids were young, I barely read, let alone wrote. But through all those years, God was giving me stories. Stories that played out only in my mind, until that day He called me to write for Him.

We never know what God has in store for us. Or how He might use our past mistakes to shape and strengthen us. We simply have to cling to His promise "to prosper and not harm us, to give us hope and a future."

If you've read any of my other books, I hope you enjoyed revisiting Ouray as much as I did, seeing what's happening with old friends and meeting some new faces along the way. In real life, Ouray is located in southwestern Colorado and is known by many names—the Switzerland of America, the Gem of the Rockies, the Ice Climbing Capital of the United States and the Jeeping Capital of the World.

As always, I would love to hear from you. You can contact me via my website, www.mindyobenhaus.com, or you can snail mail me c/o Love Inspired Books, 233 Broadway, Suite 1001, New York, NY 10279.

Wishing you many blessings,

Mindy

REQUEST YOUR FREE BOOKS!

2 FREE INSPIRATIONAL NOVELS

PLUS 2
FREE
MYSTERY GIFTS

Love Inspired®

LII5

SPECIAL EXCERPT FROM

When a young Amish woman must choose between two very different brothers, will she find the husband of her heart?

Read on for a sneak preview of
THE AMISH BRIDE
The first book in the brand-new trilogy
LANCASTER COURTSHIPS

"I'm glad you came for ice cream, Ellen. I wanted to talk to you. Alone," Neziah said.

"*Dat!* Look at me!" Asa cried from the playground.

"I see you!" Neziah waved and looked back at Ellen. "Well, not *exactly* alone," he said wryly.

He continued. "I wanted to talk to you about this whole courting business. First, I want to apologize for my *vadder's*—" He shook his head. "I don't even know what to call it."

"You don't have to apologize, Neziah. My *vadder* was a part of it, too," she told him. "I know our parents mean well, but sometimes it might be better if they didn't get so…*involved*."

He smiled and looked down at his hands. "My father can sometimes be meddlesome, but this time I think our fathers might have a point."

Ellen looked at Neziah, thinking she must have misheard him. "You think…" She just stared at him for a moment in confusion. "You mean you think our fathers have a point in saying it's time we each thought about getting married?"

He met her gaze. He was the same Neziah she had once thought she was in love with, the same warm, dark eyes, but there was something different now. A confidence she hadn't recalled seeing on his plain face.

"Yes. And I think that you and I, Ellen—" he covered her hand with his "—should consider courting again."

Ellen was so shocked, it was a wonder she didn't fall off the picnic table bench. This was the last thing on earth she expected to hear from him. The warmth of his hand on hers made her shiver…and not unpleasantly. She pulled her hand away. "Neziah, I…"

"The past is the past," he said when she couldn't finish her thought. "We were both young then. But we're older now. Wiser. Neither of us is the same stubborn young person we once were." He kept looking at her, his gaze searching hers. "Ellen, I was in love with you once and I think—" he glanced at his boys "—I think I'm still in love with you." He looked back at her. "I *know* I am."

Don't miss
THE AMISH BRIDE by Emma Miller
available September 2015 wherever
Love Inspired® books and ebooks are sold.

Love Inspired®

Love the Love Inspired book you just read?

Your opinion matters.

Review this book on your favorite book site, review site, blog or your own social media properties and share your opinion with other readers!